He leaned back against his desk and crossed his arms in front of his chest. The smile he wore conveyed his admiration.

"Interesting. Smart, fiery, yet still able to retain your composure in tense situations. I'm truly impressed. I must say, my mother really outdid herself. Do me a favor… the next time you see Norma Jean, and she asks how her ingenious plan went, tell her this for me." His arms snaked out and yanked Milán to him. He held her in an unyielding embrace as his lips clamped down on hers.

He felt Milán try to wrench herself free, but she was no match against his strength, or his irritation. He would teach his mother a lesson once and for all, and if he had to use her latest protégé to ram that point home so be it. With adept movements, Adrian slid one of his hands up and into her hair at the base of her neck to hold her steady. His other arm moved to encircle her back. He leaned over her, tilting her body backward in order to deepen the kiss. Time slowed and then screeched to a halt as he continued the onslaught on Milán's mouth with deft precision.

The kiss ended unhurriedly. He took his time unlocking his lips from hers. Unable to help himself, he gave one final nibble to her bottom lip before moving his hand to her face. She tasted like nectarines. His thumb that caressed the swollen flesh was slightly unsteady. "Tell my mother I said 'nice try,'" he spoke in a voice thick with emotion, "an...

Books by Lisa Watson

Harlequin Kimani Romance

Love Contract

LISA WATSON

is a native of Washington, D.C. Her romantic imagination is fed by the city's historic and political backdrop. Her hobbies are as eclectic as her music collection, but what Lisa loves the most is writing strong, positive characters that are memorable to the reader and fun. Lisa is enamored with scenic beauty, and the picturesque locales she visits always seem to find a way into her latest novels. An asset-management analyst, Lisa is a subcontractor to ATF (Bureau of Alcohol, Tobacco, Firearms and Explosives), and the copublicist for the *RT Book Reviews* annual RT Booklovers Conventions. She helps promote the bestselling national and international authors that attend the conference via local media outlets. Lisa has been married for sixteen years and lives in the Raleigh, North Carolina area, with her husband, two teenagers and Maltipoo, Brinkley.

Want to connect with Lisa? Contact her at lywatson007@hotmail.com, on Facebook (NCLisaWatson) or Twitter (@lywatson007).

LOVE
Contract

LISA WATSON

HARLEQUIN® KIMANI™ ROMANCE

For Leslie Esdaile Banks, my literary friend,
and sister "Glamazon." Thanks for the laughs, sage advice
and friendship. Rest in peace.

Recycling programs
for this product may
not exist in your area.

ISBN-13: 978-0-373-86304-4

LOVE CONTRACT

Copyright © by Lisa Watson

Printed in U.S.A.

Dear Reader,

What fun I had creating the characters in this novel! Beforehand, I imagined the confusion and humor that could arise from a mother's matchmaking plans gone awry. Norma Jean Anderson's son, Adrian, is livid at her scheme to set him up on yet another blind date. But, when he first lays eyes on the smart and fiery Milán Dixon, their chemistry is explosive. I wanted them each to leave an indelible impression on the other, but for totally different reasons. Milán sees a missed job opportunity. Adrian sees red! His ex-fiancée's infidelity makes him resist giving his heart away again, much to his mother's dismay.

I hope you enjoy reading my debut Harlequin Kimani Romance. I'll be working on the next story in The Match Broker series soon, so stay tuned to see who Norma Jean will match up next!

Be inspired….

Lisa

Thanks to Kimberly Weeter of Kimberlys-Kreations.com. One of my best friends, and real-life staging and interior design expert.

To LBJM—Thanks for always making me laugh.

To Halden Lopez-Llizo for making sure I got my thoughts right—in Spanish!

Chapter 1

Adrian Anderson surveyed the array of suits in his walk-in closet. With a critical eye, he chose a dark gray Armani with a double-breasted jacket. His selection included a crisp white shirt and patterned silk tie. He was picking out shoes when his telephone rang. He padded across the floor of his master suite and checked his phone. *Mom.* Sighing, he tried his best to channel what little patience he had left as he picked up his cell phone. "Good morning, Mother," he said as upbeat as he could manage.

"I said I was sorry," she began without preamble. "How long do you plan on staying annoyed with me?"

"That would depend. How long do you plan on fixing me up with mental patients?"

"Sweetheart, I know you're upset, but there's no way I could've known she was in therapy."

"Mom, please. Therapy I can handle, but this chick called her doctor all through dinner. Do you know how weird that was?"

"Adrian, don't dramatize it," his mother admonished.

"You weren't there." Adrian sighed. "Let's not go over this again, okay? You pleaded your case last night—several times I might add. When are you going to get the point and stop matchmaking?"

"When you find the right woman and settle down," his mother huffed. "Which would be sooner than later if you wouldn't fight me at every turn."

Adrian pinched the bridge of his nose. His mother was driving him as crazy as his date, Cynthia. He'd dubbed her the Cyber Stalker. She'd called his cell phone and left numerous texts since their disastrous date.

It was always the same. Any date orchestrated by Norma Jean Anderson—also known as the *Love Broker* by all his close friends—ended in disaster.

Each time he got wrangled into one of his mother's hookups, he would add the woman to his contact list. If the date ended badly, the woman in question would get a nickname that easily stood out on his phone. This trick ensured he didn't answer a call by mistake. So far, this system worked like a charm. Now, if he could get his mother to find another hobby.

"Mom, you've been at this longer than I've been in business."

"And look how successful that's been. You're doing well for yourself, honey. Business is thriving, you're a pillar to the community, handsome and smart. All you need is a wife to share your life with."

He ran a hand over his stubbled jaw. "The last trip I almost made down the aisle didn't turn out too well, remember?"

There was a short pause before his mother said, "I know, honey, but you can't let the indiscretions of one woman ruin your chance for a happy life."

"Indiscretions? You're being much nicer than that gold digger deserved. She slept her way through half of my friends, and almost had me saddled to her unfaithful butt for the rest of my life. Luckily for me, I interrupted that last romp before she became a married woman. So now I've got an ex-fiancée and ex-friends. Trust me, I'm better off not giving another woman a chance to break my heart and wreck my bank account."

"Adrian, I know she hurt you. Believe me, I get it. But that was over a year ago. If you let that woman scar you for life, she wins. It's time you got back in the saddle again. Stop going through women like you do dress shirts and let me find you one that will love you unconditionally."

"Tell me again what's natural about this? I'm a grown man whose mother is trying to control his love life."

"Adrian, if I wait for you, I'll drop dead before I get to see you become a father."

He sighed into the phone. "You'll be a grandmother—one day. Until then, my life is fine the way it is so please humor me and butt out," he said with a chuckle.

"I'll butt out when you say, 'I do,'" his mother replied with humor. "We'll discuss this later. Your dad's taking me to breakfast so I've got to run."

"Mom…"

"Have a great day, honey," Norma Jean said quickly and hung up.

Adrian set the phone down. When his day started with a disagreement with his mother, it only got progressively worse; and recalling how the love of his life had duped him days before they were to marry hadn't helped his mood.

"Great," he muttered. Ripping the damp towel from his middle, he tossed it in the general direction of his clothes basket.

With angry strides, he headed toward the bathroom as if he were on his way into battle instead of work.

Turning in front of the mirror, Milán Dixon decided she liked the finished product. The navy blue suit was one of her favorites and it never failed to boost her confidence. A neutral blouse, classic diamond earrings and navy pumps completed the ensemble.

"You'll knock him dead," she said to her reflection before winking at herself. After eight weeks and so many job interviews she had lost count, Milán was more than ready for the tide to turn. Her decision to start fresh in a new city had come as a shock to her close-knit family, but she was adamant on leaving Miami. Thanks to her now ex-boyfriend, Eduardo Vega, Milán was left with a lot of bad memories and the debt to go with it.

Finding out that the beach house, antique cars and money he had flashed were just a facade was the worst day of her life. Eduardo's latest real estate plan of buying homes with his investment partner and flipping them had tanked right along with the market. Then she had found out that his investment partner had been his overindulgent father. Thanks to a sobering conversation with Senor Vega, Milán had discovered that the man she had loved and trusted was a liar, and that his father was pulling the plug on financing his son's ill-considered pursuits.

Two weeks later, Vega's lawyer had phoned Milán to let her know that Eduardo was cut off and on his own. The only things his father's money had not paid for were the furnishings she had purchased to decorate their new home and a few of their joint credit cards.

When Eduardo had come home that night, she was more than ready for him. Armed with the newly discovered facts, Milán had baited him into talking about the sweet deals he had in the pipeline, and how wonderful their life together was going to be. When she could stand it no more, she had blindsided him with his father's confessions. At first he had attempted to deny and explain them away, but eventually he had become angry and accused her of breaking his trust.

Milán had shot back that he should be happy she wasn't breaking his nose. As if on cue, her family had arrived. Her mother, Pia Aragon Dixon, had circled Eduardo like a lioness ready to defend her cub. Her father, Vincent, and sisters Nyah and Elena had been close behind. Seeing that he was outnumbered, Eduardo had told her she wasn't worth this and walked out. That was the last time she'd seen him.

Humiliated and now homeless, Milán had decided to get as far away from her heartbreak as possible. She had packed up everything she owned, settled the joint accounts she had shared with Eduardo and found a rental home in Chicago. With a modest nest egg in her savings account, and the last two paychecks from her job, Milán had tearfully bid her family goodbye. With promises that she would check in regularly, Milán had gotten into her loaded-down car and hit the road.

It had been a whirlwind of activity ever since. Arriving at her new home, a vintage loft apartment in the heart of Chicago's Lakeview neighborhood, Milán dove into decorating her new place and making it her own. The hard work soothed her frazzled nerves and broken heart. She could mourn her failed relationship with Eduardo later. Right now she wanted to concentrate on finding a job, learning her way around Chi-Town and paying off the rest of what she owed their creditors.

It took a few weeks, but Milán was finally acclimated to her environment. She still hadn't received any job offers, but she remained hopeful. Though she had not met many people, the ones she had become acquainted with were great. While at a church function with a neighbor, she had met Norma Jean Anderson and immediately connected with the older woman. Meeting Norma Jean seemed like the answer to her prayers. Just listening to her gush about her real estate mogul of a son, Adrian, was a step in the right direction. With him looking for an interior designer and stager to compliment his agency, and Milán in need of a job, Norma Jean assured her that working there would be the perfect match.

It sounded exciting enough, and Milán was eager to start work. Some of the prospects had been hopeful and she'd received a few callbacks, but so far nothing had panned out.

Sweeping all the younger woman's concerns aside, Norma Jean had promised to arrange a meeting for her with Adrian. Milán got caught up in her new friend's excitement. She was confident all would work out. *This would be a job made in heaven,* she had thought the very day Norma Jean had called back and told her to be at his office the following Monday at nine-thirty.

Coming out of her reverie, Milán took a deep breath. "It's all yours," she told her mirrored reflection. She retrieved her purse and portfolio off the coffee table. "This is your time to shine, *chica.* He'll love your designs and ideas and will offer you a job," she said confidently. Glancing at her watch, Milán frowned. Being late for her meeting with her soon-to-be boss would not look good. It had to be a fantastic interview. Juggling her purse, coffee and briefcase, she headed out.

After seeing all the traffic she had to contend with, Milán was glad she'd decided to leave early. It was definitely a wise move. Downtown Chicago during rush hour was bumper-to-bumper. By the time she had arrived and parked at the North Halstead

address Norma Jean have given her, she had less than twenty
minutes to spare. Her gaze traveled up the brick boutique-styled
building. She definitely liked the large windows and glass door.
A dark blue banner with white letters read Anderson Realty.

"This is the place," she said aloud. Giving herself a mental
shake, she squared her shoulders and went in.

Chapter 2

Adrian sat heavily in his chair. He felt like his head was about to explode. The throbbing in his temples made it difficult to concentrate on the woman standing in front of him. When his assistant had come in to tell him that his nine-thirty appointment was waiting, he had assumed it was a prospective interviewee for the Interior Designer position. How wrong he had been. When Adrian's assistant told him that the woman he had agreed to meet with had been recommended by his mother, a feeling of dread rippled through his entire body and then pure anger. Interior Designer indeed. This was no interview. It was a setup.

In an effort to calm down, he ran his hand over his face and breathed deeply. Resentment made the air hiss on its way out of his mouth. His mother had gone too far this time. This was his place of business, not some bar. With a practiced eye, Adrian scrutinized the woman that his assistant had shown into his office. He may be mad, but he sure wasn't blind. She was like a stop sign placed in the middle of a freeway during rush-hour traffic. Her looks demanded a man come to a screeching halt and take notice. Long legs did an excellent job of supporting her curvaceous body. The golden hue of her skin was flawless, except for a splattering of freckles on her upper cheeks and nose. Her hair was the color of rich chocolate, and with golden highlights. The way light reflected off the luminous waves that hung just below her shoulders made the color contrast stunning. It beckoned a man to run his fingers through it. His hands clenched together unconsciously.

Adrian's gaze sought hers. This time the air that expelled itself from his mouth was for an altogether different reason. *Those eyes.* Her eyes were the pièce de résistance. They were an expressive, medium brown with flecks of light gold around the outer edge that held both strength and mystery. They could drown a man if he was not careful. *And he would love every minute of it,* he told himself. Adrian felt an instant reaction to the visual display of beauty before him. Instinct kicked in. His body eagerly anticipated taking the perusal to a whole new level, until he remembered the person responsible for the exquisite vision standing in front of him. Cold water splashed on his face could not have produced a faster effect. Slightly annoyed that he had gone poetic at a time like this, he remembered the catalyst by which this gorgeous woman now graced his presence. *I can't believe this. She's done it to me again.*

That realization was enough to jolt Adrian out of his trance. His ardor was quickly squelched and back under wraps where it belonged. This time when his eyes centered on the woman before him, they brooked no warmth. "I can't believe she sent you."

"Who?"

Despite his new motivation to send her on her way, Adrian couldn't deny that her voice was as appealing to him as warm butter on a biscuit—and he loved biscuits.

"My mother!" The two words burst forth, coating the air with tension. He tried to calm himself. Lord knows it took considerable effort. It would appear that the Love Broker had struck again. Looking at the latest proof of Norma Jean Anderson's handiwork made his blood pressure skyrocket. Hadn't they had this conversation hours earlier?

Confusion registered on the woman's face. "Well, yes. Your mother gave me your card and told me I had to come see you." Sitting across from him, she shrugged out of her suit jacket. "She told me you were exactly the man I needed."

"I'll bet she did," he quipped. Adrian stood up, his hands straightening his suit. He'd heard enough. She may be working it in all the right places, and his temperature may have risen a degree or two, but there was no way in hell he was taking the bait. *No way.* "Listen, Miss?"

"Dixon...Milán Dixon."

"It would appear you've wasted your time, Miss Dixon—and mine. As fine as you are, and believe me you are without a doubt the most desirable woman my mother has ever paraded my way, I'm just not interested. Of course, if she had tried a few months ago before I got inundated by trolls maybe I would've—"

"Excuse me?" Despite her surprise, Milán scowled at him. "You think this is a...a come-on?"

Though his eyes devoured her, they also held a hint of challenge that transferred itself to his tone of voice. "Like it isn't?"

Milán was out of her chair with her hands on her hips in an instant. "No, it isn't. This was supposed to be a job interview."

Her rapid breathing caused her ample chest to stretch the ecru-colored silk blouse taut. His eyes were drawn to the motion like a magnet on a stainless steel refrigerator.

Coming around the expansive desk, Adrian stopped just shy of wearing her. He was impressed she stood her ground. It would appear his mother had finally found one with spirit. "Oh, my mother set up an interview all right, but it's apparent from the looks of you a job was the last thing she had in mind."

Standing ramrod straight, it took a few seconds for Milán to recover. When she did, her voice chilled the air around them like a cold front. "You know, of all the stuck-up, asinine, incredibly rude men I've come across in my travels, you, Mr. Anderson, set the precedent."

He leaned back against his desk and crossed his arms in front of his chest. The smile he wore relayed his admiration. "Interesting. Smart, fiery, yet still able to retain your composure in tense situations. I'm truly impressed. I must say, my mother really outdid herself. Do me a favor. The next time you see Norma Jean, and she asks how her ingenious plan went, tell her this for me." His arms snaked out and yanked Milán to him. He held her in an unyielding embrace as his lips clamped down on hers.

He felt Milán try to wrench herself free, but she was no

match against his strength, or his irritation. He would teach his mother a lesson once and for all, and if he had to use her latest protégé to ram that point home, so be it. With practiced movements, Adrian slid one of his hands up and into her hair at the base of her neck to hold her steady. His other arm moved to encircle her back. He leaned over her, tilting her body backward in order to deepen the kiss. Time slowed and then screeched to a halt for him as he continued the onslaught of Milán's mouth with deft precision.

The kiss ended slowly. He took his time unlocking his lips from hers. Unable to help himself, he gave one final nibble to her bottom lip before moving his hand to her face. She tasted like nectarines. His thumb that caressed the swollen flesh was slightly unsteady. "Tell my mother I said nice try," he spoke in a voice thick with emotion, "and Lord knows I do mean nice."

Adrian reluctantly stepped back so that he could look into Milán's face. He expected to see her all doe-eyed and flushed. Instead her eyes bored into him with heated purpose. Her jaw was clenched so tightly the lips he had so expertly ravished seconds before were thinned to mere slits.

"Release me," she ground out. "Now."

Instantly, she was free. A second later, Milán delivered a well-placed fist to his midsection. Adrian's world faded momentarily, but not before he saw the expression of satisfaction that slid across her reddened face.

Caught off guard, he sagged against his desk. It took some time, but eventually the pain dulled and he was able to stand up straight. He took a few deep breaths. "I take it you didn't like my message?"

Milán reached over to grab her jacket off the chair, and a portfolio out of her briefcase. She flung it on his desk, and left. Stopping before she got to the door, Milán spun around to look at him. "If you ever put any part of your anatomy on me again without my permission, I promise you I'll cut it off. Oh, and just so you know, your mother said you were looking to add an interior designer and staging expert to enhance your practice. Considering the real estate market we're in right now, that was a wise choice on your part. Regrettably, Mrs. Anderson didn't warn me in advance how rude and unprofessional her son was—not to mention being a narcissistic jackass. Had she done so, I could've saved the price of parking."

Adrian winced when his office door slammed with such force it sent one of his numerous Realtor awards crashing to the floor. A good minute passed before he gingerly lowered himself into his chair. *Breathe.* He told himself. His ears were still ringing with the censure of Milán's words. The last part of her insult had been in Spanish, but that didn't matter. He was fluent in Spanish and understood every word she'd said. Even if he hadn't, the intonation translated perfectly. Inches away, her résumé taunted him. Either he'd just made a monumental error in judgment, or his mother wasn't taking any chances on making Miss Dixon's claim believable.

Figure the odds of your being wrong, his conscience piped in. *Not after all you've dealt with over the years.* Still, what if he was? The familiar throbbing returned to his temples. It would have to wait. The pain in his stomach took higher priority.

"Huh," he said, incredulously. "I just got cursed out in two different languages, and by a complete stranger. I guess it's safe to say this day couldn't possibly get any worse."

Later that afternoon, his assistant knocked and immediately entered his office.

"I'm sorry to interrupt, Mr. Anderson, but I've been trying to buzz you."

"I don't want to be disturbed." Adrian's bad mood had resurfaced after lunch. He had found out from one of his employees that a potential client had decided to sign with Tony Ludlow, one of his major competitors, to list his penthouse apartment on Lake Shore Drive. Finding out he had lost a sale always bothered him, but hearing that Ludlow had taken one of his clients from under his nose irked the crap out of him.

"You have a call holding, sir."

"Let me guess, my mother's on the line checking on her latest coup?"

The woman opened her mouth to reply, but Adrian interrupted.

."You'd think she'd give me some time between setups to catch my breath and regroup. When will she learn?" Agitated, he rose from his chair to pace around the room.

"Oh, let's not forget my date this past weekend. She made calls to her therapist all through dinner. Now there was a woman in touch with her inner self. Or how about the kleptomaniac that eyed my Rolex more than me? If I'd have married her, she'd be stealing her own damned silver!"

"You know…I can see you're busy so I'll just leave you in peace. One of the other Realtors can take the call." She backed out and closed the door firmly behind her.

Startled, Adrian halted his diatribe to stare after her. *What had he done?*

Thoughts of Milán came barreling back. He could see her horrified and then livid expression after he had kissed her. He hadn't been prepared for the venom she had hurled at him. Another thing he didn't see coming was his body's reaction to their kiss.

He felt like he'd been jolted with an electric current. The feeling had run through his entire body before settling like an explosion into his groin. That woman felt altogether too amazing in his arms. Her body was enough to disrupt any man's peace of mind, and that temper of hers only enhanced his excitement— until she had punched him.

You ruined your chances and there's no recovering from that fiasco, he complained to himself. Adrian was thoroughly embarrassed and disgusted with himself over his actions. Not that he'd ever admit that aloud. He stifled a curse. It was time to call it a day. The sooner he ended his backward day the better.

While stacking papers into his briefcase, he spotted Milán's folder. Staring at it, he was about to throw it away when curiosity overpowered him. He grabbed the portfolio, sat down and put his feet up on his desk. Several moments later, the reality of the situation hit home. "*Estúpido,*" he said to himself. After reading over Milán's credentials and seeing samples of the homes she had staged, he was intrigued, impressed and extremely pissed off. He was stupid. She was just the caliber designer he needed at Anderson Realty and he'd blown it.

With a multitude of services under the Anderson umbrella, Adrian's goal was for his clients to be as unstressed as possible during their realty experience. His clients ranged from average income to really-rolling-in-it kind of wealthy, but a realty company wasn't enough; Adrian had a title company, real estate attorney, a relocation expert, a mortgage specialist and concierge dedicated to providing whatever services were needed. Adrian's dream had almost come to fruition, but came dangerously close to going belly up when the market bottomed out.

Now more than ever, he needed to assist his clients any way he could to combat the fierce competition. His nemesis, Tony Ludlow, came to mind. Ludlow had been in business about as long as Adrian. From the moment they had met, some undercurrent of one-upmanship had sparked and ignited. Ludlow would watch Adrian to see what he would do, or gloat when his agency came out ahead. He was sure Ludlow did not have a staging expert.

A great designer would be the proverbial icing on the cake for his company. *Like the one you just watched walk out your office. Actually stomped out was more accurate.* He had to fix this. "*¡Me tengo que disculpar!*" There was no way that he was going to let her get away without taking a good look at what she could bring to the table.

Granted, having to apologize for the huge mistake he made did not sit well with him, but the idea of losing such a talented designer to someone else appealed to him even less.

Adrian ran a hand over his face. He truly hated this part. Picking up Milán's résumé from his desk, he scanned over it. He grabbed his handset and dialed the mobile number she had listed in her contact information. The line rang twice and then connected. Her sweet, now slightly irritated voice brushed across his ear.

"Hello, Miss Dixon. This is Adrian Anderson calling."
Click.
"Damn," he muttered.

After a moment, he grabbed the phone and dialed another number. This time it was picked up on the fourth ring.

"Hi, Dad, is Mom around?"

Heathcliffe Anderson's strong baritone voice came over the line. "Not yet, son. It's Monday. She's at her yoga class, but should be in any moment. You want me to have her call you?"

Adrian grabbed his briefcase and jacket. "Not necessary, Dad. I'm on my way over. Mom and I have something to discuss in person—and it's long overdue."

While Milán drove home, she attempted to cool off. When she was distraught about something, two things gave her tranquility: driving her car with the music blaring and cleaning the heck out of something. She wasn't home yet, so driving would have to do.

What a jerk! She replayed her encounter again in her head. Her fingers flew up to her lips. *How dare he kiss me!* Just thinking about the encounter made her heart race, but she was confused. Norma Jean had spoken so glowingly of him. She couldn't help getting caught up in the excitement, too. Jeanie believed that the two of them would make a great team. His mother couldn't have been more wrong.

After she had left Adrian's office, the reality of her situation was driven home. She needed a job, and she needed one soon. She refused to dip into her savings account more than necessary. Her parents had gifted their children with a small monetary umbrella to use for a rainy day. Granted, this was more like a torrential downpour, but there was no way she was touching that money unless it was a dire emergency. She would simply double her efforts to find employment. Now thanks to that narcissistic playboy her morning was wasted.

Just thinking about their run-in got her blood boiling all over again. Her cell phone rang. She checked the number and saw it was her mother. There was no way she could talk to her right now. She was too upset and her mother would pick up on it. Neither Milán nor her sisters could keep anything hidden from Pia Dixon. Besides, Milán wasn't ready to recount her horrid morning with Adrian Anderson and his massive ego. Not without bursting into tears of anger and frustration. *He ruined everything!*

Chapter 3

"For the last time, I didn't have an ulterior motive," Norma Jean said with exasperation. "I suggested Milán contact you because she's looking for a job, and you're looking for an interior designer." She regarded her son from over her glasses. "Seemed a perfect fit to me."

"Yeah, like her being crazy beautiful had no bearing in sending her my way?"

Adrian's mother sat back in her chair. She stopped her scrapbooking and observed her son carefully. A knowing smile crept onto her face. "You think she's beautiful."

Adrian looked indignant. "And you didn't? Come on, Mom, you're killing me. You *knew* darn well I'd think she was gorgeous, but I recall having told you somewhere between one and a million times to stay out of my love life. Why won't you do this?" He slammed down into the nearest chair. Adrian released a loud, harsh sigh, and then gazed up at the ceiling before shaking his head.

Norma Jean resumed placing small patterned shapes across her page. "Honey, you really should calm yourself. Maybe you should take up yoga? It would teach you how to release that pent-up stress you're carrying around."

"Calm myself? How can I? I honestly never know who's lurking around the corner waiting to pounce on me compliments of Norma Jean Anderson."

"I resent that."

With a raised eyebrow he shot back, "Tell me I'm exaggerating." Adrian rubbed his hand over his face. When he opened his eyes again, his gaze traveled around his parents' family room. It looked like Cupid had set up shop and never left. Every surface had something pertaining to romance: his mother's stack of inspirational love stories, the two red his-and-her teddy bears joined at the lips on a bookcase, the rose-scented tea lights with the red heart-shaped candleholder and family photos stored in floral decorative boxes. It was a good thing she kept her walls and carpet neutral. Any other color would have clashed with her "love couture." His mother wasn't dressed in a frilly pink number right now, but she might as well have been. Norma Jean was a die-hard romantic in every bone of her five-foot-nine-inch frame.

Married to her childhood sweetheart, his mother thought everyone on the planet should be as lucky in love as her and his dad. To prove the point, she'd been fixing him up since middle school. How he'd escaped matrimony this long was anyone's guess. Frankly, Adrian thought it was nothing short of a miracle.

Taking a deep breath, he jumped back into the fray. "Mom, when are you going to understand that love isn't something you can orchestrate like one of your bingo nights at the community center? That's not how it works. That's not how *I* work."

His mother rolled her eyes. "Okay, now you're being dramatic. Need I remind you that since your breakup, your track record with superficial playthings—that don't have the wits or the foresight to be wife potential—is staggering?"

"I'm glad my heartbreak amuses you," Adrian snapped.

Norma Jean slid her glasses into her short, spiked gray hair and stood up. She pointed a well-manicured finger in her son's direction. "Don't you use that tone with me, or so help me I'll put my women's safety classes to good use and drop you on this floor."

Adrian was instantly contrite. "My apologies."

His mother smoothed her hands over her knit jogging suit and returned to her plush chenille chair to resume her scrapbooking. A minute or two later, she glanced up to find Adrian still brooding.

"Honey, believe me I was only thinking of your company when I sent Milán to you. I know how hard it's been for anyone trying to make a living in the housing market these days. Besides, you're always so stressed out about that Ludlow man getting one up on you."

"I'm not stressed," he refuted.

"Call it what you will," she continued. "The point is I saw a perfect opportunity to help you so I took it. And if you'll recall, since Justin got married last year—to the blind date that I had arranged for you by the way—"

"I was there, Mom, remember?"

"Like I was saying," she elevated her voice and pressed on. "I may have set you up on a date or two since then, but I've respected your right to find your own wife. No matter how long and drawn out that process seems to be," she added. "What I don't understand is why you're so against my choices—or yours for that matter. You date someone once or a few times and then poof. They vanish into thin air. Everyone's been kicked in the teeth by love, son. The trick is to get back on that horse and gallop."

Adrian stared at his mother. "It's not that I'm against marriage or a serious commitment. I envision myself with a wife one day, but I refuse to enter into another long-term relationship without knowing exactly what I'm dealing with. I won't make that mistake again. Ever."

She shook her head. "I might as well resign myself to the fact that sooner or later I'll have to rent some grandbabies."

He snorted. "Now who's being dramatic?"

As much as he hated to admit it, she was right. That matchmaking scheme his mother had set in motion had forced him to stand up his blind date, Sabrina Ridgemont, in an effort to teach his mother a lesson. Unbeknownst to Adrian at the time, his best friend, Justin Langley, had gone to break the date, in person. Through a series of events, Justin had led Sabrina to believe *he* was Adrian. The fiasco that ensued gave Adrian a headache just thinking about it. Fortunately, the outcome was what mattered. The truth had come out eventually, and despite a rocky start, Justin and Sabrina were now happily married. *Thanks to Norma Jean and her machinations.*

"Okay," he conceded. "I apologize for jumping to conclusions about your friend. Now can we change the subject? It's true, I would like a designer on staff to give my clients' homes an edge, but I doubt Milán Dixon will be the one."

"Oh?" his mother queried. "I don't see why not. She's perfect."

She is most definitely perfect. Suddenly, Adrian looked uncomfortable. "Because I screwed up big time. I thought... Suffice it to say, when I saw her, I assumed you were up to business as usual and that it wasn't a real interview. I let her know point-blank what I thought of her—and your interference."

"Adrian," his mother gasped. "Tell me you didn't embarrass me."

He recalled the scene in his office. "You don't know the half of it," he mumbled.

Norma Jean shifted in her chair. "Now I raised you better than that."

He held his hands up in front of him. "Please, no sermon. I've already been properly chastised today—in two languages."

"Well good." She nodded approvingly. "You deserved it. I recall her telling me that she was bilingual. What language does she speak?"

"Is that relevant?"

His mother arched her eyebrow.

"Spanish," he grumbled. "She speaks Spanish."

Humph. "You learned the language to increase your client base. This would have been a perfect arrangement. If you ask me—"

"I didn't."

"You got off light," she finished. "I can't believe you botched the meeting. You need to call her and apologize."

"I tried."

"And?"

"And, as soon as I told her who I was, she hung up."

"Serves you right, but you have to try again."

"Mom, she knows my phone number now. The next time she won't even bother to pick it up." He eyed his mother. "Unless…you can—"

"Forget it. You messed this up, now you're going to find a way to fix it. I'm not bailing you out."

Adrian's eyes bugged out. "Need I remind you that you were the one that put me in this position to begin with?"

"I merely presented you with an opportunity. Your big mouth made you blow it."

"What's all the ruckus?"

Both turned to see Heathcliffe coming into the room.

Norma Jean brightened at seeing her husband. "Hi, honey."

"Long story, Dad."

His father leaned against the closest wall. "So give me the condensed version."

"Our son insulted Miss Dixon, put his foot in his mouth, and got blessed out in the process."

"Thanks for the recap," Adrian drawled.

Norma Jean flashed a smile. "No problem, sweetie. Anyway, Cliff, I merely suggested he make amends for being loud—and wrong."

"Sounds good to me. I mean if he—"

Adrian sat up. "Am I not sitting right here?"

His parents resumed their conversation.

After a few moments, Adrian threw in the towel. Getting up, he kissed his mother before walking over and patting his father on the shoulder. "I'm leaving now. I know when to call it quits."

"I guess that's true. It has been a rather long, eventful day for you, hasn't it?"

Adrian nodded. "Dad, you have no idea. Mom, I'll be over for dinner on Thursday, okay?"

"Tell me something I didn't know," Norma Jean joked.

Before Adrian got to the door, his mother's voice stopped him. "Wait a minute."

Adrian turned. "Yeah?

"Since you know Spanish, why didn't you just answer her?"

For the first time today a smile lit up his face. "And ruin that exit? Not on your life." Adrian winked.

"Scoundrel," his mother called after him.

When Adrian left the room, Heathcliffe settled himself in the seat his son had vacated and went back to discussing things with his wife.

Realizing he'd forgotten to ask his father something, Adrian headed back into the family room. He stopped dead in his tracks when he heard his dad say, "Okay, Jeanie, fess up."

Silently, Adrian crept out into the hallway and stood there waiting to pounce.

"Cliff, I'm sure I have no idea what you're talking about."

Heathcliffe scrutinized his wife. "You set him up again, didn't you?"

That got Adrian's attention. He leaned forward to hear his mother's confession.

"I told you both, I only suggested Milán contact him for a job. No more, no less."

"Jeanie?"

"She's a nice young woman that I met in church through a mutual friend—"

"And that's it?" her husband interrupted.

Adrian saw his mother shoot his dad the *look*. Despite being worried that he might have been duped, he was glad not to be on the receiving end of his mother's pique.

"Like I was saying," Norma Jean continued. "Milán mentioned she's looking for a job as an interior designer. Naturally, I thought of my baby. What's the harm in that?"

"Nothing, darling, as long as that's your only reason for bringing them together."

"Oh, please. I haven't involved myself in Adrian's love life in forever. I'm not about to start now," she huffed returning to her project.

Heathcliffe got up and leaned over his wife. When they made eye contact, he flashed Norma Jean *his* look. She blushed when he kissed her soundly. "That's my girl."

That was Adrian's cue. The last thing he needed to see was his parents making out. There had been enough disasters today without adding that bit of horror.

Stealthily, Adrian headed for the entrance. He was completely wrong about his mother. A huge grin began. For once in Lord-knows-how-long, she had respected his wishes to stay out of his love life. He was satisfied that his dogged determination had finally paid off. The good humor was short-lived when his thoughts returned to a hot-blooded Amazon beauty he had ruthlessly insulted. *Great, you've prevailed in the war with your mother,* he told himself. *But how are you going to win the battle with Milán?*

Later that evening, Milán raised her yellow-rubber-gloved hand to her forehead to wipe the sweat away. Returning to scrubbing her counter, she increased her efforts. "The man's an idiot, Nyah," she complained to her sister over the speakerphone. "I didn't think they had men left that full of themselves. What, do they take aside boys that show the most potential when they're young and program them to be self-absorbed idiots? I'm telling you if they do, Adrian Anderson got in line twice. You should have heard all the things he said to me. I swear he's lucky that all I did was walk out. I felt like breaking something over his arrogant piñata head!"

"Will you calm down?" Nyah Dixon pleaded.

"No, I will not. I'm too pissed to calm down. *El me besó,* Nyah."

"*¿Qué?*" Her sister shrieked. "*¿Por qué?*"

"Because he thought I was some stupid matchmaking setup. He thought his mother sent me and wanted to prove a point. I showed him my point," Milán said hotly. "He's lucky I didn't land it farther south."

"Oh my. No wonder you're in a cleaning frenzy."

"*No lo soy,*" Milan lied.

"Honey, I can hear the exertion in your voice over the phone," Nyah replied. "Clearly, you're scrubbing the heck out of something. Not that it surprises me. You always take out your frustrations on your house, or whoever's house you're in at the time. *Cada vez que te disgustarse, te conviertes en un limpiador obsesivo.*"

"I do not," Milán protested. "There's nothing obsessive about my cleaning."

"Uh-huh… *¿Qué aspecto tiene?*"

Milán halted scrubbing and straightened up. "*¿Qué dice?*"

"You heard me."

"What do you mean, what does he look like? What's that got to do it?"

"*Responde la pregunta.*"

Exasperated, Milán let out a loud sigh. "He was too obnoxious for me to tell. After he made me mad, I didn't pay much attention."

"I'm not buying that," Nyah said, firmly. "Come on, tell me."

Milán groaned. "Must we do this now?"

"*Deje de darle vueltas al asunto y dime. ¿Buen besador? ¿Hace que el corazón palpite solo mirarlo? ¿Es alto?*"

Milán groaned. "I didn't ponder if he was a good kisser or not and no, my heart didn't flutter. It was racing, but that's because I was angry. And he's tall. At least six foot two."

"Athletic, or really muscular?"

Milán paused. "Somewhere in the middle. He's definitely in shape."

"What about the rest of him? What color are his eyes? Does he have a strong jaw? What about his skin? Is it a warm caramel, luscious milk chocolate or soft delectable nougat?"

Unable to help herself, Milán laughed. "Why do you always compare men's attributes to some kind of sweets?"

"I don't know. I just love desserts. It's my second favorite pastime."

"Men being the first," her sister replied.

"Yes, now speaking of which—"

"Fine," Milán interrupted. "Yes, he's good-looking. Very— and he knows it which is a definite turnoff, second only to his overbearing personality. His skin was like…desert sand at sunset. His eyes were like Oloroso sherry. A warm, vibrant brown that was very expressive." Her breath caught in her throat as she remembered their ill-advised encounter. "His body was... firm in all the right places. There's no doubt he works out often. And...he tasted like...hazelnut coffee."

Nyah snorted. "Hazelnut coffee? Didn't pay attention, huh?"

Milán frowned against the phone. "It wasn't like that. I can appreciate the physical attributes, while disliking his arrogant nature and superiority complex. Trust me there was nothing impressive about that."

Worked up just remembering Adrian's behavior, Milán went back to cleaning. The scrubbing continued, but this time on a quieter scale.

"*¿Oye, puedes aguantar esperar? Tengo otra llamada telefónica.*" Milán clicked over when she heard a beep. "Hello?"

Silence ensued. "Hello?" Milán repeated. When nobody spoke up, she clicked back to her sister. "*Lo siento.*"

"*¿Quién era lo?*"

"*No sé.*"

The line beeped again.

"*Un momento,*" she said to her sister as she clicked to the second line. "Hello? I can hear you breathing, you know," she told her caller. "Fine," she snapped and returned to her sister.

After another few minutes, her line beeped again.

"This is getting ridiculous," Milán complained.

"*Hablarémos después,*" Nyah replied and hung up.

"Look, I don't know who taught you phone etiquette, but—"

"Miss Dixon, wait. Don't hang up. This is—"

Milán's expression darkened upon recognizing the voice. "I know who it is," she said coldly. "Your rudeness is becoming legendary."

"I'm sorry about that. My battery was going dead on my phone so I switched."

"I see." Her voice was laced with skepticism. "So how did you get my number?"

"Your résumé."

She grunted in response.

"I'd like to speak with you, if now is a good time?"

A long bout of silence ensued.

"Just a few minutes," he persisted. "That's all I'm asking."

Milán leaned against the kitchen counter. "I don't think that's a good idea, Mr. Anderson."

"Why not? Are you afraid to talk to me?"

"Ha," she laughed in his ear. "Nice try, but I don't rise to bait that easily."

"I don't suppose you'd be willing to call me Adrian, would you?"

"No."

"Fair enough. The reason I'm calling, Miss Dixon… What is that?"

"What is what?"

"That noise?"

Frowning, Milán stopped scrubbing the inside of her refrigerator. "Nothing." She closed the door as quietly as she could, and then set the cleaning supplies down. She moved to the far side of the room. "You were saying?"

"Anyway, what I called to say is that I wanted to…apologize…for my…behavior earlier today. It was uncalled for and I was wrong to jump to conclusions like that. I'd like to make it up to you."

"You don't do that very often, do you?"

"What?"

"Apologize."

"No."

Despite herself, Milán's lips curved into a smile. *At least he was honest. Boorish, but honest.*

"So am I forgiven?"

Her eyes widened. "Hardly. You kissed me—without my consent."

"I know. I was out of line."

"You think?" she snapped. "Besides, your apology didn't sound genuine. Try again."

"Fine, it would appear my heartfelt sincerity—"

She couldn't help the snort that escaped her lips. "Heartfelt?"

"Sincerity," he continued, "isn't enough for you. So tell me how I can make amends?"

"To be honest, I'm not sure. Apparently you're used to getting your own way—even when you're wrong."

"That's hardly a fair assessment," he countered.

"According to whom?"

"Okay, Adrian Anderson apology—take two. Miss Dixon, I got caught up in my own personal issues earlier and took my frustrations out on you. It was rude, unprofessional and I apologize."

Milán peeled her rubber gloves off one at a time. "Yes, it was."

"So, am I forgiven?"

"No, you're not."

"Will you come back for a proper interview?"

"I don't think so, but I appreciate the phone call."

"Wait," Adrian said, quickly. "I really think we should meet face-to-face to discuss this."

"Not a snowball's chance, Mr. Anderson, but if I change my mind, you'll be the first to know." She hung up. *Serves him right.* Sliding her gloves back on, Milán grabbed her sponge and returned to scrubbing the hell out of her kitchen.

"Well, that went well," Adrian groused. He put his phone down and headed into the kitchen. Practically ripping the door off its hinges, he bent over to scan the contents of his fridge. Grabbing a beer, and a mound of other things, he pushed the door shut with his leg and set his bounty on his granite island.

"What's for lunch?"

Adrian glanced up to see his best friend walk into the room. He scowled. "I don't remember hearing the doorbell."

"When have you ever heard the doorbell?" Justin Langley washed and dried his hands. He walked over to a nearby cabinet and retrieved a small plate before sidling up to the counter to fix himself a sandwich.

"Back in the day, people got shot for less."

"We're not out on the range or in a saloon," Justin countered not the least bit intimidated by his friend's foul mood. "So I think I'm safe."

With a flick of his wrist, Adrian popped the top off his bottle and took a long pull on his beer. "I wouldn't count on it."

"So, who pissed you off?"

"Long story," Adrian groused.

Justin pulled up a bar stool and sat down. "I'm all ears."

Chapter 4

Adrian stared at the metal locker in front of him. This was not exactly the afternoon he had in mind. He wanted to enact his plan to get Milán to agree to his job offer, not stand in his gym for a weekly basketball game with Justin.

He'd called Milán several times over the past few days, but after the first two messages Adrian decided against leaving others. At that point it was obvious she wasn't planning to call back, and he didn't chase after anybody.

In truth, Adrian was annoyed he couldn't convince her that Anderson Realty would be a great match for her. When he'd casually asked his mother about Milán, Norma Jean sweetly informed him that she was not keeping tabs on the woman. *A lot of help she'd been,* Adrian complained to himself. Any other time his mother would've had Milán's GPS coordinates mapped out with her next destination already calculated. Now all of a sudden she was tight-lipped and didn't want to interfere?

He had to admit that Milán was on his mind for nonwork-related reasons, too. At the most inconvenient times, he'd think about what happened in his office. His body would stir each time he recalled the feel of her body pressed against him, or the warmth of her full lips as they brushed against his own. She may not have wanted the kiss, but there were moments when he was sure she'd been participating. He tossed that thought aside. Maybe that was wishful thinking on his part. She had punched him after their kiss had ended, so clearly it wasn't that memorable on her end. Still, that brief encounter with Milán had intrigued him more than any of the last few he'd had with women.

"Hey, did you just get here? You aren't even changed."

Adrian spotted Justin walking toward him. He retrieved his clothes from out of his bag. "No. Just preoccupied." He nodded at Justin before he stripped out of his work clothes and changed into his basketball gear. "What's up with you?"

"Same old, same old," Justin replied while getting dressed. "How are things with Senorita Dixon?"

"How would I know? I haven't spoken to her since the day we met."

"What are you going to do about it?"

"At the moment nothing, so drop it."

"Fair enough," Justin replied. "So, what's the latest with the Love Broker? The guys think she'll have you fixed up again by summer."

"Not gonna happen."

They walked toward their reserved court. Adrian set his towel and water bottle on a bench. "She has officially stopped butting into my love life."

Justin looked skeptical. "Since when?"

They walked to the top of the key and got in position. Adrian bounced the ball so that Justin could check him.

"Since she and I had it out and called a truce." He did a spin move around Justin and threw up a bank shot. "There's been no more interfering. She hasn't tried to fix me up since Cynthia."

Justin caught the ball under the net and they switched places. "The Cyber Stalker, right? Come on, man, do you honestly think your mom is going to give up trying to get you married?" Justin dodged past him. "She's just lulling you into thinking she's changed. She'll wait till you least expect it and then, bam!" He slam-dunked the ball for effect. "Blind date."

Adrian took the ball. Justin checked him and Adrian shot past him and hit a fadeaway. He let out a loud whoop and pointed to the basket. Justin rolled his eyes.

"Dating can wait." Adrian walked over to the bench to get his water. "I've got to convince Milán to join the firm."

"I thought you'd let that go?"

"You know I don't take no for an answer…at least not for long."

"Good to know. I'll be sure and tell Dent-in-her-grill Donna. She'd be thrilled to hear you've changed your mind."

Adrian let out a loud chuckle. "About wanting her? Hell will turn into a lovely condo community first."

"There are thousands of interior designers in Chicago," Justin reasoned. "What makes her so special?"

"Beats me," Adrian countered. Just then his mind conjured up an image of her locked in his embrace. He wiped his face with his towel. "Just an instinct that tells me she's the one I want."

Justin regarded his friend closely. "For the company or something personal?"

"Strictly work," Adrian specified.

"You sure?"

Adrian bent down to retrieve the ball. "Dude, I have enough stuff going on right now without entanglements of the feminine persuasion."

"By the time the Love Broker gets done with you, you won't know what hit you."

Frowning, Adrian rubbed the sweat off his face and neck with the front of his jersey. "I'm telling you, Mom said there were no ulterior motives and I believe her. Besides, I've got the perfect plan to get what I want."

Justin stared at him. "What plan?"

"Dad was complaining about all the cleaning Mom has him doing. You know, how it's interfering with his TV shows. He let it slip that Milán's coming over for dinner this Saturday."

"Why?"

"Because Mom's taken a liking to her, plus she's new in town. It's the perfect way to get some face time in and convince her to work for me."

"You think she will? You already blew the first hookup."

"It wasn't a hook up," Adrian shot back.

"Oh, right," Justin laughed. "More like a setup."

Adrian glared. "It'll look like a chance meeting. We'll clear the air and I'll convince her that Anderson Realty is the logical choice."

Deciding to call it quits, they retrieved their stuff and headed to the locker room.

"I hope things work out according to plan."

Adrian fell into step beside his friend. "Of course it will. I came up with it."

Justin's expression was skeptical. "Yeah, that's what I'm afraid of."

Three days later, Milán was driving down a tree-lined street checking house numbers as she went by. She smiled when she saw one house had an array of garden gnomes displayed across the grass. For some reason just seeing the miniature ceramic people as decorative art always made her giggle.

When she spotted the house, Milán eased her car into a vacant space at the curb. Her practiced eye roamed appreciatively over the inviting home. She parked, grabbed her purse and climbed out of the car.

She took a bag from the backseat and walked confidently toward the front door. Balancing the items in her hand, Milán rang the doorbell.

Seconds later, the door opened and a tall man smiled at her. "Hello, you must be Milán."

"Hello, Mr. Anderson." She held out a brightly colored bag.

He took the proffered gift and stood aside to let her enter. "Thanks and welcome."

"Cliff," she heard Norma Jean yell at the top of her lungs. "Will you get the darn door?" Milán stifled a laugh.

"You should hear her sing," he joked. "Here, let me take that for you."

Milán eased out of her cardigan. Her gaze traveled around the foyer as she stood there. She noted the polished wood floor, creamy yellow walls and the profusion of plants. From what she could see, the historic bungalow-styled house was spacious and bright. "You have a lovely home."

"Thank you. Now let's go find my beautiful siren."

Milán followed behind him to the kitchen. She watched him poke his head through the door. "What happened to 'honey'?" he said, sweetly.

His wife didn't bother to look up from her task. "That's when you answer the door the first time I ask you. Now will you get it before our guest decides to go next door for dinner?"

"No need, I caught her before she went over there," he teased.

His wife turned around. When she spotted Milán, she wrinkled her nose at her husband. "You're incorrigible." Norma Jean walked quickly to the doorway and hugged the younger woman tightly. "How are you, Milán?"

"I've been better, but I'm hanging in there."

"Job search going slow?"

"Yes, but I'm hopeful something will turn up soon. Thanks for inviting me to dinner, Norma Jean. It was just what I needed. I've been so intent on sending out résumés lately that I'm starting to feel like a bona fide hermit."

"We're happy you could make it, and don't worry. I just know you'll be getting a callback soon. You just have to stay positive."

"That's the plan."

"Come in and make yourself comfortable. Dinner's almost ready."

Heathcliffe handed his wife Milán's present. Norma Jean peeked into the bag and squealed with delight.

"Banana pudding," she exclaimed. "Thanks so much for bringing it."

"My pleasure. It's one of my favorites, too."

She watched Norma Jean place the dessert in the refrigerator. "Dinner smells delicious."

"Honey, let's hope it tastes that way," Norma Jean chuckled.

After putting the finishing touches on her signature mashed potatoes, and sautéed whole green beans, Norma Jean opened the oven door to check on her beef roast. "Just a few more minutes," she informed the lucky roast.

"Can I help you with anything?"

"No, thanks. You just relax. So, how are you liking Chicago? Are you settled in?"

"It's fantastic. I'm renting a loft on West Aldine. I love the exposed brick walls and timber ceilings. Still getting used to the weather, though."

"Lofts are pretty popular," Heathcliffe interjected. "I prefer a place with walls that actually go up to the ceiling."

Norma Jean stirred her gravy and then tasted it. "I agree with Cliff, but being a designer, I'm sure you've already put your personal touches on it."

"Just about." Milán laughed. "Jeanie, are you sure there's nothing I can do?"

"Not at all, honey. You make yourself comfortable."

"May I use your restroom?"

"Sure." Norma Jean turned to her husband. "Cliff, would you mind?"

"Not at all." He ushered Milán down the hall to the powder room.

On the way back, the family room window caught her attention. Walking over, Milán peeked into the backyard. Flowers in an array of vibrant colors were everywhere. Suddenly, Adrian popped into her head. Milán's expression mirrored her confusion. *I just don't get it,* she told herself. *How can two wonderful people like Norma Jean and her husband have such an obnoxious son?*

"That's a mystery," she said quietly. She shook her head in disgust. "Thank God I don't have to deal with him anymore."

On cue, Adrian's face manifested before her. Not the irate-looking Adrian, but the one that had kissed her senseless; the one whose eyes were alive with desire, whose body was smooth and hard like granite. The one that ran his thumb over her lips after he'd practically branded her with his own. *Stop it,* she scolded herself. He's a playboy that delights in wrapping women around his finger.

"Well that won't ever be me," she vowed. Disturbed, Milán pushed thoughts of Adrian aside. She was about to head back to her hosts when the sound of a loud crash followed by a commotion drifted down the hallway

Milán rushed into the kitchen. "Is everything okay?" she said quickly. "I…I heard a crash."

"I'm sorry, dear." Norma Jean's cheeks turned a faint red. "I was startled and dropped a dish. I'm fine."

"Hello, Miss Dixon."

Milán whirled around to see Adrian standing near his father.

"What are you doing here?" she blurted out.

Before he could reply, his mother spoke up.

"It would appear my son will be joining us for dinner. Oddly enough considering today is Saturday—and not Thursday." She smiled serenely in his direction.

"Yes, that's true." Adrian returned his mother's wide smile. "I usually come for dinner on Thursdays."

"Good to see you no matter what day it is," his father chimed in.

"Thanks, Dad."

He turned toward Milán. "Imagine my surprise at finding you here." Adrian closed the distance between them. When he leaned in, his voice was a taunting whisper. "And look…it's not even snowing."

Surprise was evident in Milán's wide-eyed stare. She was silent so long, Adrian's parents turned in their direction.

"Milán? Are you okay?"

"Yes," she said, quickly. "I'm fine, Jeanie. I just…didn't…" She turned a baffled expression toward Adrian. "I didn't expect to see you again, much less so soon."

"I have a habit of popping up where I'm least expected."

"That's an understatement," Norma Jean shot back.

"You're right about one thing, Mr. Anderson."

"Really? What would that be, Miss Dixon?"

A tempered expression crossed her face. Milán stepped forward to speak in a voice only he could hear. "There are no snowballs to be found. What a pity."

Chapter 5

Norma Jean glanced between the two of them. "Here, honey." She handed her son the bowl of potatoes. "Adrian was just about to tell me how this all came about when you walked in."

Milán watched Norma Jean push the bowl forcefully at Adrian. She bit back a chuckle.

The bowl connected with his chest. With a questioning glance toward his mother, he took the side dish into the dining room.

When he returned, he was lightly rubbing his chest. "I was telling Dad that I was in the area showing a house to a client."

"Really?" his mother inquired, sweetly. "Where?"

"Farther down on North Melvina."

"What a small world," Norma Jean commented before she left the kitchen and took more food to the table.

The moment Adrian's mother was gone, Milán rounded on him. "I don't buy that for a minute."

He regarded Milán with amusement. "Excuse me?"

"What you told your mother. I don't believe it."

Unable to help himself, Adrian moved closer. "First of all, you don't know me well enough to automatically accuse me of lying."

Milán snorted loudly. "Don't I? They say you can tell much about a person's character in the first few moments of meeting them."

"So what makes you an expert?"

"Experience. Though, I didn't heed that advice in my own

life until it was too late. The results were disastrous, and something I'm not inclined to repeat."

"If we'd just met, in addition to you obviously being a poor judge of character," he countered, "I could say that you're a, hothead that can't hold her temper—and a poor kisser."

A gasp escaped Milán's lips. "How dare you," she said indignantly. "You think you can take what you want without consequence and everyone is supposed to fall in line and do your bidding? You're so conceited it's appalling."

With a shrug, Adrian leaned against the sink. "I tend to stray from doing the expected. Tell me, Miss Dixon, why do you think I'm here?"

"What?"

"You don't believe my explanation, and since you're an expert, you must have a theory."

"I hope it's not one of those dates your mother likes to fix people up on. If it is, she's wasting her time. I've sworn off egotistical men."

He snickered. "This is hardly a date. If it were, it would be the most hostile one I've ever been on."

"Well then I guess you're just here to ruin my evening."

He couldn't help but smile. "You think I was so unable to resist your alluring personality, I found out you'd be here and rushed right over under the guise of being in the neighborhood?"

The condescending tone in his voice grated on Milán's nerves. She glared at him. "Yes."

"Now who's full of themselves?"

"Normally I'm a very nice person, except when I'm insulted by complete strangers and accosted in their offices."

His smiled faded. "I didn't accost you, and I tried to apologize if you recall."

"You verbally assaulted me, and kissed me without my permission. Then you give me some lame, stammered-over apology and you think I'm supposed to be okay with that? I don't know what kind of women you're used to dealing with, Mr. Anderson, but I am not some simpering idiot who can't see past that insincere smile you pasted on your face."

"It wasn't my fault. I thought it…you were a setup. My mother's always fixing me up. I just assumed you were her latest manipulation. I'm trying to make amends, Miss Dixon, but it's difficult when you're not trying to see this for what it was—an honest mistake."

Milán crossed her arms over her chest. "Both of us being here will be a disaster. I think one of us should leave."

A lazy smile started at the corner of his mouth. "I guess you could—if I make you that uncomfortable."

Her eyes darkened. "Nothing you do makes me uncomfortable."

As if a gauntlet had been tossed, Adrian pushed away from the sink and sauntered toward Milán. He didn't touch her, but she took a few steps in the opposite direction anyway.

"Are you sure about that?"

"Yes."

Adrian lowered his voice to barely a whisper. "So you haven't thought about our kiss not once since you left my office?"

Milán paled. "*Your* kiss, Mr. Anderson, not mine and no, I haven't."

A smug look crossed his face. "I don't believe you, Miss Dixon. My guess is you did, and just thinking about it makes you…uncomfortable."

Her head tilted slightly to the side. "Then you'd be mistaken," she replied sweetly. "A bruise to that overinflated ego of yours no doubt, but I'm sure you'll get over it. Besides, I'm not a good kisser, remember?"

Before he could retort, Norma Jean sailed into the kitchen.

Milán wondered if Adrian's mother was either oblivious, or purposefully ignoring the tension coating the air like melted caramel on an apple.

"I'm thrilled you two are getting along so well," she commented. "You know, I honestly had my doubts whether you would after Adrian—"

"No point rehashing that again, Mom. I'm sure Milán has forgiven me that minor mix-up." His eyes held a hint of challenge. "Isn't that right, Miss Dixon?"

"So, how was your showing?" Milán asked, not bothering to answer his question.

"Great," he replied, playing along. "The couple seemed very interested. The house is all brick, has upgrades galore and custom hardwood floors with cherry inlays. They'll probably make an offer."

"Have we moved dinner in here?" Heathcliffe inquired, coming through the kitchen door.

Norma Jean motioned everyone to the table. Adrian held out his mother's chair while his father assisted Milán. Minutes later, Heathcliffe was about to say grace when the doorbell rang.

"You expecting anyone else, sweetheart?" he asked his wife.

"Not that I'm aware of."

Adrian rose from his seat. "I'll get it."

He excused himself and left the room. When he opened the front door, Justin was standing there.

"Cutting it close, aren't you?" he whispered.

"In-law insanity," Justin muttered.

When his wife reached the landing, he put an arm around her waist.

Adrian kissed Sabrina on the cheek. "How are you, Brina?"

Sabrina Ridgemont Langley returned Adrian's quick peck and followed her husband inside.

"Just fine and you?"

"Never better. We're just starting dinner."

"What?" Sabrina's eyes widened with dismay. "Oh, dear. Justin saw your car and wanted to stop and say hi. We should've called first." She backed up, tugging on her husband's sleeve as she went. "Give our regards to everyone, okay?"

"He'll do no such thing," Norma Jean called from behind Adrian.

"You two lovebirds come right in and join us. We've got plenty. I've made a roast and my signature mashed potatoes." She winked at Justin.

"Music to my ears, Ms. Jeanie."

"If you're sure—" Sabrina began.

"You know I love company, and this is turning into a real dinner party."

After everyone was settled, Norma Jean made introductions and then asked Adrian to get two more place settings. He was trying to locate cloth napkins when Milán came in.

"Your mother asked me to get another trivet."

Adrian retrieved the napkins from an upper cabinet. "Sure," he told her.

He walked across the room, grabbed one from a drawer and handed it to Milán.

"I was more than capable of getting it."

"I'm sure you're very capable in whatever you do," Adrian drawled.

She rolled her eyes before snatching the trivet from him. Milán started to leave and stopped. A brief expression of uncertainty crossed her face. How the night had unfolded was causing her a moment of suspicion. What had started out as her coming to a casual dinner had turned into an event. Was Jeanie really trying to set her up with Adrian? *No, it couldn't be,* she told herself dismissively. Her new friend may be a matchmaker, but there was no way she'd ever date a man like her son.

"Are you okay?"

Blinking, Milán realized Adrian was staring at her. She cleared her throat. "Yes, I'm fine," she assured him. Turning on her heel, she quickly left the room.

Dinner was lively. Everyone took turns contributing to the conversation.

Milán turned to her hostess. "This is a fabulous meal, Jeanie."

"She's outdone herself as usual," her husband praised.

Sabrina gave Milán a nudge. "Jeanie excels at three things. Cooking, bringing a crowd together and fixing people up."

Everyone nodded in agreement and the table buzzed anew with comments. Milán observed Adrian being noticeably quiet.

"Oh, don't mind him," Justin told her after following her line of sight. "He's been fixed up more by his mother than he's sold houses."

Milán's gaze returned to her plate.

Adrian rolled his eyes. "Quit exaggerating."

"I'm just saying." Justin laughed. "It's been a lot."

"An awful lot," Sabrina chimed in.

"A whole lot." His dad chuckled getting in on the fun.

Adrian shifted in his seat. "Okay, we get it."

Milán directed her attention to Justin. "So what you're saying is none of them were ever a love connection?"

"Oh, there've been plenty of love connections," Heathcliffe alleged. "Just not for Adrian. Isn't that right, son?"

When she pressed for details, a collective groan went around the table. Milán glanced at Norma Jean with curiosity.

"It's a long story," Norma Jean began.

"Mom, do we really need to bore Milán with details?"

She smiled at her son. "We most certainly do."

Norma Jean recounted how she'd arranged a date with her best friend's niece, Sabrina, but Adrian stood her up. Justin picked up the story from there.

"So naturally, I couldn't let him do that," he said with a laugh.

"Naturally," Adrian said, drily.

"I went to the restaurant to break the date on his behalf."

"And before I knew it, he'd assumed Adrian's identity," Sabrina added.

"But didn't you know Justin wasn't him?" Milán queried.

Sabrina shook her head. "How could I?"

Milán stared at Adrian. "You didn't contact her before the date? You know, to break the ice?"

Adrian shrugged. "I wasn't planning on going so there was no point."

The expression Milán gave him could've melted steel. "You should've told her the truth and canceled the date like a gentleman."

The table was silent for a moment before Sabrina said, "It's amazing everything worked out in the end. Actually, we should thank my ex-boyfriend who happened to show up right then. He was a real jerk."

Milán's cool expression settled on Adrian. "Apparently, he wasn't the only one."

"Uh, anyway," Sabrina continued, "he came over and introduced himself."

Justin turned toward Milán. "I couldn't tell him my real name before I'd told Sabrina the truth so I told him I was Adrian."

Milán gasped, waving her hands excitedly. "*¡Oh, Dios mío! ¡Que una aventura!*"

The table collectively looked from Milán to Adrian and back again. Adrian's expression was unreadable.

"Perdóname," Milán apologized. "I said, what an adventure."

"It certainly was," Sabrina agreed. "I didn't know you were Spanish."

"I'm not. My mother is Mexican, and my father is African-American. My parents insisted we grow up bilingual."

"That's fantastic," Sabrina replied. "Do you have brothers and sisters?"

"Two sisters, Nyah and Elena. I'm the oldest."

"It's great you're fluent," Sabrina complimented. "I barely passed French. You know Adrian—"

"Knows all about Milán being bilingual," he interrupted. "I got a sample of the lovely senorita's Spanish when we met," he informed the crowd.

Justin and Sabrina shot glances at Adrian, but he didn't make eye contact.

"So, what happened next?" Milán inquired, missing the exchange.

"They fell in love and are living happily ever after." His mother sighed happily.

Adrian stood up and began clearing dishes off the table. "See? It turned out great for everyone. Now who's up for dessert?"

"You all relax," Norma Jean told the group. "We'll be right back."

Adrian followed her into the kitchen. As soon as they cleared the doorway, Norma Jean punched him. "What are you really doing here?" she demanded.

Chapter 6

"Ouch." Adrian grabbed his arm. "What was that for?"

"You're lying."

Adrian rubbed his arm. "I'm getting really tired of hearing that. I told you. I was in the area, and since when has my showing up out of the blue been a surprise?"

Norma Jean placed her hands on her hips. "Oh, please, you were just here two days ago, Adrian. Like you had no idea we'd invited Milán over tonight for dinner. What kind of game are you playing?"

"None."

Norma Jean looked skeptical. "I'm your mother, remember? I know when you're lying to me. If you're trying to pull the wool over my eyes, you'll need to do better than this. I mean really, son, this isn't even original."

"Okay, detective. Tell me how I'd know Milán was here when I haven't spoken to you since I left that night?"

"You're resourceful, you tell me." Going to the refrigerator, Jeanie retrieved the banana pudding and then the bowls from the cupboard.

Adrian regarded his mother while he gathered spoons from the silverware drawer. "Fine. You don't believe me, I get it, but Justin and Sabrina dropped in, as well. Are you going to punch them in the arm, too?"

"Don't be silly," she chided. "And why are you acting like you don't speak a lick of Spanish?"

"Hey, she assumes I don't speak her language so why bother to change her opinion? And what's with the inquisition?"

"Is that what you think this is?"

"It's kind of hard not to. Two weeks ago you were trying to get Milán and me together. Now you're throwing kitchen knives at me with your eyes across the table."

"I was not," she protested. "I was trying to help you for work—nothing more. You botched things up so badly when you met, the last thing I want is her thinking I set her up."

He laughed heartily. "Since when?"

Norma Jean rolled her eyes.

The evening had definitely not gone according to plan. Adrian was used to being the topic of discussion in a crowd, just not in a negative light.

"It's a moot point anyway," he reasoned. "Thanks to that roasting I got out there a few minutes ago, Milán probably thinks I'm a jerk."

Norma Jean's expression softened immediately. She walked over and touched his arm. "Honey, you know that wasn't our intent."

"Could've fooled me," he groused.

"Adrian, at some point you need to realize you're making a big deal out of nothing."

He closed the distance between them. Adrian hugged his mother and gave her a peck on the cheek. "That may be true, but now isn't that time."

Norma Jean opened her mouth to call after him, but abruptly closed it. A questioning look crossed her face. Suddenly, she laughed aloud. "Fascinating."

After dessert, everyone pitched in to clean up. Milán felt right at home rolling up her sleeves and helping out amid a throng of people. Justin and Sabrina took turns discussing past exploits and dating horror stories, prompting Milán to touch on a few debacles of her own ending with Eduardo. She was surprised to find that the sting she felt thinking about their breakup had subsided.

When they were done, the Langleys decided to leave. Milán hugged them both.

"It was great meeting you, and Justin."

"Likewise," Sabrina told her.

Adrian walked his friends to the front door. He was about to open it when Sabrina cornered him. "Why did you stop me from telling Milán you speak Spanish?"

"Was that what I did?"

Sabrina's eyes narrowed. "You know darn well that's what you did." She pointed a finger in his chest. "I know you, Adrian. You never do anything without a reason. What are you up to?"

"I've heard that a lot this evening." He bent down and kissed her on the cheek. "I promise you I'm not up to anything."

"That suave thing doesn't work on me. I'm not going to go all gaga and forget that you haven't answered my question," she informed him.

"No, that only works when I do it." Justin laughed before gently guiding his wife out the front door.

Sabrina dug her heels in at the threshold. "I mean it, Adrian. You'd better not do something to Jeanie's new friend that I as a woman might personally take offense to."

Adrian placed a hand over his heart. "You have my word."

Before she could reply, her husband maneuvered her onto the porch.

"I owe you one," Adrian said jovially.

"You got that right." Justin closed the door behind him.

Adrian returned to the kitchen to find Milán offering to help put the food away.

"You have helped enough for one evening," Norma Jean announced. "You and Cliff go out and enjoy the deck. Adrian will help me with the leftovers."

She glanced between them with uncertainty. "Are you sure, Jeanie?"

"Yes," she smiled, reassuringly. "We can handle this."

"We?" Adrian called from the doorway.

"Yes, we," his mother stressed.

Adrian arched his eyebrow at that. When Milán turned to

face him he replaced the shocked look with a grin and said, "Of course."

Once they were through, Norma Jean shooed him out of the kitchen.

"You go on. I'll put coffee on and be out shortly."

By the time Adrian slid the door open and stepped onto the deck, Milán and his dad were deep in conversation. He took a minute to observe the two of them unseen. He couldn't help but watch how the breeze kept blowing her hair across her cheek, or how she continually swept it out of her way. After a few times, she opted to pull it securely behind her ear. He was only half listening to something his father was saying, but tuned in each time Milán laughed or spoke.

A keen eye when it came to observing people, Adrian could tell if an action was sincere, or contrived. Listening to Milán as she interacted with his father, he knew without a doubt that the interest she showed his dad was genuine. Oddly, that made him smile.

He stepped into view. "It's nice out tonight."

"Sure is," his father chimed in. "I was just telling Milán about Chicago winters."

"She's from Florida, Dad. I don't think she's all that anxious to hear about our frigid temperatures just yet." He regarded her for a moment. "Coral Gables, right?"

Milán's head snapped up. "Yes. How'd you know that?"

"I read the résumé you left and checked your references. You received your BFA and Master's degree in Interior Design from the Miami International University of Art and Design. After graduating you interned at an architectural firm and did some freelance projects and received your accreditation as a professional staging expert. From there you were hired at a well-known firm in Miami before going to work at a company in Coral Gables. Your past employers spoke very highly of you, Milán. Your design portfolio is very impressive, as well."

She was unable to hide her surprise. "Thank you."

Heathcliffe pushed away from the railing. "I'd better go in

and help your mother finish up. She may say she doesn't need it, but if I don't at least offer, I'll hear about it later," he chuckled and then went inside.

Adrian sat down on one of the benches stretching his legs out in front of him.

"I'm sorry about the kitchen run-in. I seem to rub you the wrong way, don't I?"

"It appears you go out of your way to do so, Mr. Anderson."

"That's not my intent," he admitted. "Miss Dixon, would you do me a favor?"

Milán lowered herself into a chair across from him. "It depends. What is it?"

"Would you please call me Adrian? You're killing me with the Mr. Anderson thing. It's starting to make me feel as old as my father."

She stared at him a few seconds before she conceded to his request. "Fine."

Their eyes locked. He raised an eyebrow after a few moments and waited.

"Adrian." She smirked.

"Thank you." His eyes twinkled with mischief. "Was that so hard?"

"Evidently not." She studied him, suspiciously. "So, were you *really* just in the neighborhood?"

"Here." He retrieved his cell phone from his pants pocket. He pulled up the calendar and held it out. "See for yourself."

Milán saw his calendar and the entry listing that afternoon's appointment for a showing.

"Fair enough," she capitulated.

He put the phone away. "So you believe me when I say this was strictly a coincidence?"

"Yes, Mr. A—Adrian," Milán corrected. "I believe you had an appointment, not that you coming over was a coincidence."

A smile enveloped his face. "Well, it's a start."

"So your mother sets you up with Sabrina and she ends up falling for Justin instead. That's quite a story." Milán's hand eased up to her mouth to hide her smile.

A moan escaped his lips. "We aren't going to go over that again—are we? Didn't I get painted with a slanted brush enough for one evening?"

Milán arched an eyebrow. "You did that job justice all by yourself."

Adrian looked skeptical. "Really? When?"

"The day we met."

"Touché. Our first meeting was a verifiable disaster. I fully admit that I was a consummate ass that day. You'd be happy to know it got progressively worse from there. See, I apologized for all to hear."

Milán's gaze traveled around the deck and back to him. "It appears we're alone. How convenient for you."

"I promise you the next time there are more people in the room I will openly admit that I made a fool of myself. Trust me. I'd take this concession if I were you. It doesn't happen too often."

Chapter 7

Milán stared at Adrian with avid curiosity. "What? You admitting that you made a fool of yourself? Or that you were dead wrong?"

A devilish glint appeared in his eyes. "Take your pick. Neither one is a regular occurrence."

"You're very cocky, you know."

"So you've told me. I admit I've got a healthy appreciation for my abilities. What's the harm in that?"

"In small doses nothing, but you seem to think all women share your opinion."

Adrian couldn't contain his lazy smile. "Let's just say that's more rule than exception."

"Careful, your narcissistic side is showing again."

His laughter ricocheted around the small space. "You know I hate when that happens."

This time Milán couldn't keep the laughter at bay. She chuckled right along with him. When their gazes locked, she cleared her throat. "During the discussion at dinner I realized that your behavior the day we met may have been…warranted."

Adrian rested his elbows squarely on his knees. "Still, regardless of what my mother did, I shouldn't have taken it out on you. How about we start over? We didn't get off on the best foot. I'd like to correct that."

"Since your mother and I are friends, I think it would be better if you and I weren't at odds with each other all the time, so, yes." She smiled. "Let's start over."

Adrian visibly relaxed. "Great. So, how goes the job search?"

Milán shrugged. "It's fine. There've been a few prospects. I have another interview Friday."

"I'm sure it'll go well. Though I wish you'd reconsider and come to work at Anderson Realty."

"Do you really think that's a good idea?"

"Yes. My mother wasn't wrong. I am looking to expand my client services and I think you're just the caliber of designer I've been looking for. You would be a valuable asset to my company."

"I don't know—"

"Just say you'll think about it. That's all I'm asking—for now."

Milán was silent for a few seconds before she said, "Okay. I'll think about it."

Heathcliffe and Norma Jean came out to find Milán and Adrian debating the advantages of landscaping on resale value.

"Would anyone care for coffee?"

"No, thank you, Jeanie." Milán stood up. "I have to go."

"I'm glad you joined us this evening." Norma Jean grasped Milán's hands. "We loved having you."

"Thanks for inviting me. It was fun."

"Anytime, little lady." Heathcliffe gave her a hug. "We're huggers in this family. Hope you don't mind."

"Not at all." She laughed. "We're huggers in my family, too."

Norma Jean led her friend down the deck steps. They walked along the brick pathway that led around front. "You're welcome anytime."

Milán's eyes misted over. "I didn't realize how much I missed my family until I was here with yours."

She squeezed Milán's hand. "I bet you're as close-knit as we are."

"We are."

Norma Jean hugged her again. "Goodbye, dear."

Milán opened her eyes to find Adrian standing next to his mother. She released the older woman. "Goodbye, Jeanie."

"I'm leaving too, Mom. Thanks for dinner. It was…enlightening," he teased before kissing her on the cheek.

"You're welcome, sweetheart. We'll talk later," she warned her son.

"Yes, ma'am."

Waving to both of them, she turned and headed into the house.

Adrian held up Milán's sweater. "Dad said you left this."

"Oh. I completely forgot it." She reached out to take it. "Thank you."

"You're welcome. I'm glad you stayed."

"There was no way I'd be rude to your parents," Milán said seriously. "Besides, I can tolerate anyone for a short amount of time."

Adrian's hand came up to his chest. "That's good to know. Say, would you like to remove the knife you just slid into me?"

She laughed at his joke. "You know what I meant."

"Yeah. I'm also glad we were able to get past our differences."

"Who said we're past them?" she countered. "I still think you're way too full of yourself."

"And I still think you're a hothead, so I guess we're even."

Suddenly, Adrian's arms encircled Milán. She instantly stiffened.

"Relax," Adrian whispered in her ear. "I'm not going to kiss you." He gave her a big hug, and then released her.

"I didn't think you would," she retorted. "I just wasn't expecting it. What was that for, anyway?"

"Both our families are huggers, remember? And since we agreed to try being civil to each other, I suppose it's a way of sealing the deal."

"Thanks for explaining that. I'd hate to have to hit you again," she mocked.

Adrian followed her to the curb. His gaze traveled over her red Volkswagen Eos.

"A convertible. Somehow that's not surprising. And candy-apple red, no less."

"Actually it's called salsa red."

He opened her door. "Yeah, that's what I said."

Her eyes shot upward. "Are you ever wrong?"

"Uh, no. I don't think so—and it suits you, by the way."

She eased onto her seat as he shut the door. "Really? Something about me just screams sporty and fun, huh?"

He bent down until he was eye level with her. "Something like that."

She slid her key in the ignition and started the engine. "Considering you're never wrong, I'll take that as a compliment and say 'Good night, Adrian.'"

He stood up and moved back. "Good night, Milán. Don't forget to think about my job offer."

"When did I give you permission to use my given name?" she asked mischievously.

"Here I am taking liberties again. The nerve of me." Adrian sauntered over to his car.

"A Lexus GS 350. Hmm. I'm not surprised," she called after him.

He stopped and glanced back over his shoulder. "I take it something about me just screams luxury and impeccable style?"

She shook her head. "Actually, I was thinking vain and pretentious, but hey." Milán secured her seat belt and pulled off.

Adrian waited until she'd left before getting into his car. He couldn't explain the undeniable urge to get to know her better. To find out what was so special about Milán Dixon that made him ready to hand her a job without a moment's hesitation. He'd never done that before. His mother liking her would've been an instant strike against her—if she'd been matchmaking again. If he'd picked up on even the slightest hint of Norma Jean trying to fix them up, gorgeous or not, Adrian would've headed in the opposite direction on principle alone. His mother may be a consummate artist at finding his friends true romance, but where he was concerned it had been nothing but bedlam.

He had to admit that his mother referring Milán was obviously not business as usual. He mulled over how adamant the

Love Broker had been that her motives were pure. The question rolling around in his gut was…did he believe her? "I guess there's only one way to find out."

Chapter 8

A week later, Adrian was coming through the door of his home when he heard his telephone ringing. He strode over to retrieve the cordless phone.

"Hello?"

"Oh, sweetheart, am I ever glad I caught you."

Instantly alert, Adrian dropped his gym bag to the floor. "Mom, what's wrong?"

"Nothing, honey, I just need a ride to church."

He sighed with relief.

"Your father's not back yet, and I promised to take some dishes over for the carnival, and wouldn't you know it? My car won't start. I asked your father to—"

"Mom," Adrian raised his voice to be heard over her tangent. "It's no problem. I'll come get you. Just give me a few to change clothes."

"Can't you come over now? I'd hate to keep the sisters waiting for my contributions."

"I just got back from the gym, and I'm not going anywhere sweaty."

"Fine, but hurry."

Norma Jean had hung up before Adrian could respond. Setting the phone down, he hurried to his bedroom.

Less than an hour later, Adrian pulled up to the front of Holy Redeemer Baptist Church. "Here we are," he announced. "Door-to-door service."

His mother gave him a stare that would've made a lesser man dive for cover. "Don't even try dropping me off at the curb like some taxi. Boy, you'd better drive around to the parking lot, get your buns out of this car and help me take this food in like the child with manners that I raised."

Adrian opened his mouth, and then closed it. This was hardly the time to get into a sparring match with his mother. When it came to her, he picked his battles wisely. "Of course, Mom," he responded. He drove cautiously along the side of the church through the throng of pedestrians toward the rear parking lot.

After being ushered to a space by an attendant, Adrian parked, and was around the car before his mother had even undone her seat belt.

She nodded with approval. "Thank you, sweetheart." She kissed his cheek. "You've restored my faith in your common sense."

"My pleasure. Now where would you like me to put this?" he said, grasping the tote of coleslaw.

"Do you see that frazzled-looking woman with the clipboard? That's Sister Pearlie. You can set it down on one of the tables next to her." Norma Jean eased herself out of the car. "You go ahead. I've got to get the pies."

Adrian followed her instructions while trying not to check his watch. He wasn't staying any longer than he had to. Not that he had anything against socializing with the members of Holy Redeemer. Far from it, but invariably the conversation would head toward relationships. That meant, sooner or later, someone would inquire how he was doing in that department. When it came to his mother, that question was similar to waving a checkered flag at a drag race. She and her friends would start comparing notes on their offspring. That would cause heated discussions and that would lead all eyes to him. That was a hot seat he had no intention of being on this afternoon. He shuddered at the visual. Playing it safe, Adrian set his cell phone alarm for ninety minutes. That would give him enough time to appease his mother, and leave before he became relationship fodder.

At ease now that he had a game plan, Adrian maneuvered

around the lines of kids scampering between bright blue-and-white coolers that held ice pops, ice cream and other warm weather goodies. There was a giant Moonbounce, a dunking booth, various game stations and a merry-go-round. Adrian steered clear of them all. "Excuse me, I have a contribution," he said when he reached the picnic table.

"Thank you," a chipper woman replied.

When she turned around to take the container, the words, "You're welcome," died on his lips. He stepped back almost colliding with the person behind him. "Milán." Her name burst forth before he could stop it. A second later, he schooled his features and his expression returned to normal. "It's...good to see you again."

"Surprised is more like it," she retorted, her face identical to his expression seconds earlier. She glanced down at the food in his hand. "I'll take it."

He relinquished the bag.

"Thank you." She sat the parcel on the table. "I didn't know you'd be here."

Adrian stepped aside to let another person by. "Trust me, I didn't either. I was roped into it. My mother knows I don't like these things. Have you seen those kids playing?" He eyed his khaki shorts with concern. "I'm just waiting for someone to spill melted artificial liquid all over me."

"Relax," Milán soothed. "I think your clothes are safe. Besides, they're kids."

His expression turned dubious. "Uh-huh. Spoken like a woman that doesn't have any. My friend has a six-month-old. It's like his daughter waits until I come over just so she can throw up or smear her latest meal on me." He halted suddenly. "Unless you...I mean, you don't..."

"No, I don't have any children," Milán finished for him. "I'm perfectly happy being single and unattached."

"Sssh," he spoke, lowering his voice. "Don't let the Love Broker hear you say that. Those two words are enough to get her started."

"What? *Perfectly happy?*"

Adrian leaned in as if sharing state secrets. His eyes alight with mischief. "Heck, no, *single* and *unattached*."

Milán burst out laughing. "Your mother lives for those words, huh?"

"Like a ten dollar Starbucks gift card to a coffee junkie. Like a forty-percent-off coupon to a shopaholic. Like a—"

Milán's hands went up. "Okay, I get it."

He shrugged. "I'm just saying. The Love Broker enjoys a challenge."

Sitting down on a wooden bench, Milán glanced up shading her eyes from the sun. "Isn't she busy enough dealing with you?"

"Oh, so I'm a full-time job?"

Unfazed by his acerbic tone, Milán shrugged. "Well, she had plenty of stories at your roast the other night. Are you trying to say none of it was true?"

He took a seat next to her. His gaze held annoyance. "Trust me, if I'd known it was an ambush, I wouldn't have shown up, and to answer your question…no, I'm not going to deny it."

Milán started laughing. Finally, Adrian lightened up and joined in. "I'm glad my discomfort amuses you. I'm just surprised you didn't know."

She frowned. "Know what?"

Adrian let out a low whistle. "Wow, I thought it was pretty obvious."

"What was?" When he remained silent, she nudged him. "Tell me."

He moved closer, just inches from her face to whisper into her ear. "That my mother loves to multitask. Despite all your efforts, I seriously doubt you're under her radar."

Before she could reply, Adrian excused himself. "I'd better go check on my mother."

Milán watched him saunter off across the grass. Seconds later, he barely missed a young boy barreling by and squirting another playmate with a water gun. When he turned around, their eyes met. The look on his face that spoke volumes. It screamed, "I told you so."

Milán waved him off. Adrian's expression was smug before he walked away.

"Quite something, isn't he?" a woman next to her said, then sighed.

Milán nodded and stood up. "Adrian Anderson is turning out to be full of surprises."

"Don't I know it." The elderly woman grinned. "I'm Ms. Pearlie, we haven't been introduced yet, Milán, but Sister Jeanie told me all about you."

"She did?"

"Of course." She wound her arm around Milán's and pulled her in close. "I heard all about your first disastrous meeting with Adrian. Poor boy, what a misguided soul he is. He's had some troubles with women, let me tell you, but now he avoids long-term relationships like the plague. I tell you if ever a man needs to be settled down, that one does, but considering the last go-round, I don't think he ever will."

Milán couldn't help but notice this was the very thing Adrian had complained about. She was all ears now. "You don't say?"

"Oh, goodness, yes." Ms. Pearlie leaned in closer. "It's not my place to mention it, but Adrian was engaged once. Poor boy got taken for a ride. He hasn't been the same since. If you ask me, I just think he hasn't met the right woman yet. I know Sister Jeanie tries, but let's face it. Some of the women she's set poor Adrian up with were horrible. Walking disasters in skirts. I don't blame the poor boy if he's a little skittish now. Would you?"

Milán was still trying to digest the tidbits of information that the elderly woman had imparted. Adrian had been engaged, but it had ended badly. She could definitely relate to a relationship not turning out as expected. Realizing Ms. Pearlie was awaiting an answer she said, "Of course not. Granted our first meeting was a bit disastrous—"

"Like I said," Ms. Pearlie chimed in.

"True, but I've seen quite a different side of Adrian today. He's sort of—"

"I know, child. They call that..." Ms. Pearlie tapped her finger on lip in concentration. "I got it," she exclaimed with a broad smile. "Multifaceted."

"I'll take your word for it, Ms. Pearlie."

Milán found Adrian later holding open the flap to the Moon-bounce. The bored look he wore made her hurry over to him.

"What are you doing?" she hissed.

"What does it look like I'm doing? I got roped into helping with this thing."

"Will you put a smile on your face so the kids feel welcome? If you stand there glaring like you got roped into it, they'll pick up on that."

"How's this?" he asked fixing her with a spectacular smile that showed almost all of his teeth.

"*Bueno*, but can we turn the wattage down a little bit? Your smile is about to blind someone. We don't want them having to get slathered in sunblock just to ride this thing."

"Take it or leave it," he griped, but with a smile.

"That's it. Come on," she said taking off her shoes.

Adrian watched Milán ease out of her sandals and place them in a neat row along with the rest of the shoes. "What are you doing?"

Milán's hand entwined with his. "We're going in."

"Oh no, we're not," he countered.

"Yes, we are. You need to loosen up and have some fun."

"I'm plenty loose. I don't need a big plastic blow-up ride to prove that."

Tugging him along, Milán got herself positioned in front of the entrance. "Help me up," she cried with excitement.

"This is crazy," Adrian complained but did as she asked.

Laughing, she maneuvered herself toward the middle. "Come on," she yelled.

Shaking his head, Adrian discarded his shoes, tossed them to the side and launched himself into the Moonbounce. Gingerly, he made his way over to her. With so many kids and now Milán jumping with wild abandon, it was hard to keep from falling over himself.

Milán laughed hysterically as she jumped and spun around midair. She always landed gracefully on her feet. "Let's show these kids how it's done," she yelled out when Adrian finally reached her side.

"I think not."

"Come on, Adrian. *Viva la fiesta!*"

Chapter 9

Adrian finally got into the spirit of things and the two of them bounced for a long time. Milán laughed so hard watching Adrian try to do tricks and fall that she started hiccupping.

"You're going to pay for that," he threatened advancing toward her.

Milán shrieked and tried her best to run from him. It was so bouncy that her running looked more like an animated cartoon. She fell and bounced up and down a few times. When she stopped, Milán tried to get up but a hand clamped around her foot.

"Got you," Adrian said triumphantly.

"That's cheating," she protested trying to slither away.

Milán broke free and tried to run, but this time when she was knocked off her feet, it was by Adrian's entire body. He tackled her. Milán went down and dragged him with her. They rolled over a few times before coming to rest in a heap by the entrance door.

Sprawled on top of him, Milán tried her best to extricate herself from Adrian's arms. She slipped and her hand ended up in his groin. "Oh my gosh, I'm so sorry," she croaked. She shifted again trying desperately not to do it again. She held onto his arm instead.

"It's okay. Here, you try to get up first and I'll keep still," he offered.

"All right." Milán rolled onto her knees and tried to stand up. When she finally got to her feet she let out a whoop of excitement. "Want me to help you?" she asked Adrian.

"No, you could end up in my lap again. Not that I would mind in the least," he teased. "You try and make it for the door. Don't worry about me," he called after her. "Save yourself."

Milán giggled. She tried to concentrate her efforts on getting back on solid ground.

"Hooray," Milán shouted with joy as she slid out of the opening and back onto a flat surface.

Adrian came out a few moments later. "We made it."

"Yes." Milán smiled up at him. "I think we did rather well. Want to go again?"

"Not on your life."

They chatted amiably until Milán was called off to help with something. Adrian assured her he would catch up to her later.

More people showed up to the carnival to support the congregation's efforts to raise money for the community. The church focused the day's proceeds on aid for housing, after-school programs for their youth and classes at the neighborhood community center. Their pastor spoke briefly about the importance of their work, the success of their efforts thus far and implored more people to get involved by lending a helping hand to others through community service efforts.

Before long, Adrian and quite a few others were standing in line to sign up.

When Milán spotted him, a surprised look crossed her face. Moving closer, she overheard a woman mention that Adrian had signed up to give seminars. Before she could stop herself, she blurted out, "What kind of seminars?"

A man told her the classes were to help people navigate the real estate market by finding programs that granted money to first-time buyers for a down payment.

"So their dreams become reality."

"Exactly," one of them gushed. "I think that's a wonderful idea."

"During these tough economic times, people need all the help they can get," another person chimed in.

Unable to help herself, Milán sought Adrian out. She found him studying the selections at the dessert table.

"What are you doing?"

Adrian glanced up. "What's it look like? I'm exploring all my options."

Milán perused the table. "Are you always so cautious? It's just dessert."

He turned to her. "To the untrained eye, that's exactly what it appears to be, but to a connoisseur of after-dinner delights, the choices are far more complicated than they appear."

Milán's expression turned serious. "I can see how much effort this is taking. I must say, you surprise me."

"Why, because I volunteered to help with one of the church's outreach programs?"

She stared past him. "I admit that your signing up did throw me, but no, that's not it."

Adrian halted his perusal of the sweets to give her his full attention. Milán was compelled to return his frank gaze.

"So what is it, Milán? What about me has you so…mystified?"

Deciding on his choice, Adrian selected a dense piece of pound cake from off the table. When she remained silent, he politely excused himself, not waiting to see if she would follow.

Not missing a beat, Milán fell into step beside him. Her long legs easily kept stride with his.

Thinking back on all Ms. Pearlie had told her, she turned toward him. "You're a contradiction in terms," she continued as if they'd never stopped talking. "One minute you're insulting me in your office, and I have a clear picture of your character, and the next—"

"Then allow me to apologize—again." He stopped in front of her. "As I said, my behavior that afternoon was reprehensible. I can only attribute my rudeness to my paranoia over what my mother is apt to do next." Adrian sighed heavily. "I can never tell, and sometimes that puts me…on edge. I realize there's no excuse for how I treated you, but I hope you understand the reason for it."

The two stared at each other for several moments. It was Milán who spoke up first. "Now, you are forgiven."

Adrian squeezed her arm. "I'll have you know that was the most sincere apology I've ever given."

"I'll have you know that it loses some of its sincerity if you have to point that out."

His grin was dazzling. "Fair enough."

As if on cue, both of them burst into laughter. It took some time, but the humor subsided enough for them to resume their walk.

Milán was called off again to volunteer. This time, she made Adrian go with her. She was tasked with manning the pie booth. When Adrian discovered they'd be hitting her with pie plates filled with whipped cream, Adrian spoke up. "Now this will be fun."

A good sport, Milán agreed and was led off to the booth with Adrian right on her heels. She was given a plastic smock to protect her dress, and a cap to keep from messing up her hair. She gave the woman a thumbs-up and went to take her seat. Adrian helped her onto her perch and then went around to the front to stand with the rest of the crowd. When he saw her, he reached into his pocket and retrieved his phone. He took a camera picture of her.

"This isn't my best side," Milán yelled when she saw him snap a picture.

The patrons that purchased tickets lined up to have a turn at filling an aluminum pie plate with whipped cream, and then trying to hit Milán in the face with their creation.

Everyone laughed as person after person tried, and failed to hit her. Several people got close, so Milán was coated in several places with the nondairy dessert. "Come on," she taunted. "Nobody out there has a good enough aim to take me out?"

"I'll do it," a teenage boy said stepping up to the line. His pie plate was poised and ready. After a few moments of calculating, he drew his arm all the way back and then propelled it forward. The pie plate sailed through the air. His aim was true and in seconds, Milán's face was engulfed in cream.

The crowd cheered, laughing and praising the boy for his shot and Milán for being a great sport. After a few more contestants failed to hit their mark, Milán was let down so the next volunteer could go up.

Adrian walked up to Milán. "You were great," he praised.

"Thanks. I'm sure there are spaces left if you'd like to volunteer, too?"

Someone hosed the front of Milán with water to get the whipped cream off. When they finished, Adrian handed her a towel. "I think I'll pass." He laughed as he came around behind her to help untie her smock.

He eased it off and laid it on a nearby table.

"I'm surprised you didn't make a pie and try your luck."

"I considered it," he admitted.

Milán wiped her face off. She was about to take off her cap, when Adrian's hand stopped her. "You missed a few spots," he said quickly.

Before he thought better of it, Adrian reached up and stroked the topping off her right cheek. Then his fingers traced her eyebrow and an area on her neck. He observed Milán's shocked stare. "Are you okay?" When she remained speechless, he pulled on the towel bunched up in her hand. Slowly, it eased out of her grasp. Deftly, he wiped off more of the white cream from her ear and nose. "There," he said trying to sound at ease. It took some considerable effort. "All done."

The air around them became supercharged with electricity. Neither one moved away. Instead, each stood transfixed to their spots with the towel bunched between them.

Milán was the first to move. She cleared her throat and released her hold on the towel. "I, uh…thank you," she finally got out. "You know…for helping me."

Adrian's eyes raked over her face a final time before he spoke. "You're welcome. I think I'll go see what my mother is up to."

"Okay," she replied. She watched him move away and didn't stop until he had disappeared from view. Only then did she lower herself onto the bench behind her.

What was that just now? she asked herself. She could feel her heart fluttering wildly in her chest. Her breathing only now coming back to normal. "It's the adrenaline from getting hit in the face with pies," she reasoned. "Nothing to be alarmed about. I just got caught up in the chemical rush. No more no less." She closed her eyes and tried to calm herself. It was a mistake. Adrian's office manifested itself in her mind's eye. She and Adrian were next to come into view. She was back in his embrace, her head being anchored by his hand while his lips moved all over her face. They drifted lower, to her neck and then right above the top of her bra. *Wait a minute. When had her blouse been removed?* she asked herself.

When Adrian leaned back, she could see the desire in his eyes. The heat bored into her skin, searing her soul. It permeated everywhere until she was overflowing with the burning need to be consumed by him. To be loved by him.

"No," she cried out. Instantly, the scene disintegrated and recessed back into the shadows. The darkness faded and she was blinded by the sunlight around her. Milán bolted up from the bench. Her legs almost buckled.

"Are you all right, miss?" an elderly man asked coming over to her.

Milán blinked several times and took a few deep breaths.

"Yes? Oh, sorry, I'm fine. I must've been daydreaming," she assured him. "If you'll excuse me, I'm going to go clean myself up." She didn't wait to hear his reply. Milán practically ran into the church and to the ladies' room. Absentmindedly, she reached up and pulled the plastic cap off her head as she went. Setting it on the counter, Milán flipped the cold water on in the sink. She pooled the liquid in her hands and splashed it on her face a few times.

Taking paper towels from the wall dispenser, she patted the moisture from her skin. Only then did she look into mirror at her reflection. She looked the same. Exactly the same, but something was most assuredly different. What was wrong with her? *No sé,* her conscience chimed in. *This was no attraction, this was madness.* She went from being attracted to a suave, crazy sexy man that lied for a living to a suave, crazy sexy man that was too sure of himself, had commitment issues and dated women as often as he changed his ties. "There is no way you want anyone like that," Milán whispered to her reflection. "No way."

Chapter 10

After she'd gotten herself together and repaired her hair and makeup, Milán decided it was time to stop hiding in the bathroom. She'd go out and act like nothing was wrong. *What could be wrong?* she asked herself. *You just admitted you desire someone that might just rip your heart to shreds.*

"It's only a physical reaction," she assured herself aloud. "No more, no less."

Once Milán convinced herself she was fine, she returned to the carnival. She was conversing with a few patrons when Adrian sidled up next to her.

"There you are. I was beginning to think you'd left."

Milán glanced up at him. She tried not to see him in a new light, but it was hard. That new light would burn her to cinders if she wasn't careful.

"No, still here. I went to get cleaned up."

He nodded approvingly. "This look is much better for you."

"I agree." Milán laughed.

"I've got an idea. How about we go grab something to eat?"

She nodded. "Sounds good."

Milán walked with Adrian across the yard to the food tables. He picked up a plate with utensils wrapped in a napkin and handed it to her. After deciding what they would eat, they headed to an open table and sat down. While they ate, they made small talk.

Milán observed Adrian for a moment. "You know, I've been meaning to ask you something."

Adrian wiped his mouth with a napkin. "Fire away."

"What did you mean by 'I'm not under her radar'?"

"I meant that if you're not careful, my mother will try to fix you up, too."

"Oh that. You're too late," she confessed. "She already has."

Within seconds, both dissolved into a fit of laughter. This time Adrian laughed so hard tears rolled down his cheeks. "You can't be serious?"

"I am," she assured him.

Just then, Adrian's cell phone alarm went off.

Milán's eyes followed his movements. "What's that for?"

"Hmm? Oh, it's no big deal." He hit a button on his screen and returned the device to his pocket. He gave her his undivided attention. "So let's hear it."

"There's nothing to tell," she hedged, trying her best to dissuade him.

Adrian just sat there and stared at her.

"Okay." Milán placed a hand on her forehead. "It was a disaster. There, are you satisfied?"

"Uh-uh. That won't cut it," he countered. "I've had more than my fair share of people laughing at my expense over my mother's setups. It's someone else's turn, so start talking—and I want details."

For the next fifteen minutes, Adrian and Milán compared notes on how their prospective dates measured up. When she went into detail, he countered with some horror stories of his own.

Milán held her hand up to stop him. "Just wait, it gets better. When my last date realized I was half Mexican, he had arranged for us to go to dinner at an 'authentic' Mexican restaurant," she informed him. "The food was horrible, and to make matters worse, the mariachi band only knew one song, and kept stopping at our table every fifteen minutes to play it for us."

"Wow, that was terrible," Adrian chuckled.

Milán shivered just remembering the dating disaster. "I told you."

"Why didn't you just tell her that you weren't interested in being fixed up?" Adrian replied.

She played with the food on her plate. "At first I did, but then I wondered if I was being overly sensitive. My breakup with Eduardo really affected me. He was one of the longest relationships I'd ever had and when that didn't last…I decided to swear off men for a while. I wondered if the signs where there and I was just ignoring them. Like maybe there was something wrong with me."

"Nothing is wrong with you," Adrian said firmly. "The guy was stupid. The most important thing in a relationship is honesty. I know that better now than I did a year ago. My ex was a piece of work. Apparently, I was almost the last person to find out just how much," he said, wryly.

"Do you want to talk about it?" Milán offered.

His expression darkened. "What's to tell? I found out my fiancée was cheating on me…with several of my so-called friends right up until we were to be married. I caught her, called the wedding off and kicked her out of my house. End of story."

"That had to have been devastating for you," she said softly.

Adrian shrugged it off. "I'm the wiser for it. Now I keep things simple. No serious relationships, nothing more than casual dating. It's all I want at this stage. Besides, I'm too busy with work to worry about anything more. It drives my mother crazy because her Biological Grandma clock is ticking, but I'm not about to be rushed into another jacked-up relationship just to say I have a wife. Next time, it will be with the right woman and forever. No exceptions. Until then…"

"Nothing serious," she finished for him.

"You got that right," he said with conviction.

They talked a while longer, both genuinely having a good time swapping encounters. They were still huddled together comparing disaster dates when Norma Jean found them and announced she was ready to leave.

"Of course," Adrian replied getting up from the table. "Do you need any help with anything?"

"No, sweetheart, I've got a goody bag already packed for your father. The ladies will return my dishes at our next meeting." She turned to Milán. "I see you two are getting along nicely. I hate to break things up, but I'm a bit tired."

"Mom, there's no reason to explain," Adrian assured her.

Milán echoed Adrian's sentiment.

"Thanks so much for volunteering." Norma Jean hugged her.

Milán returned the gesture. "Great seeing you too, Jeanie, and you're welcome. I had a lot of fun."

Norma Jean moved away to say goodbye to a few people while Adrian headed to the car with her things. Milán tagged along.

After he packed things up, Adrian turned and extended his hand. "I'm glad we got a chance to talk."

"Me, too." She shook his hand. "Our conversations were… enlightening."

"That they were. Have a good evening, Milán. Maybe we'll see each other around?"

She nodded. "Maybe we will."

With one final wave, Milán left. Adrian's phone rang. Reaching into his pocket, he glanced at the screen and then answered it.

"Hey, Justin."

"I thought you were coming over to watch the game?"

"Sorry, I got sidetracked." He leaned against his car door. "I went to a carnival at Mom's church."

There was a long pause on the phone before Justin replied, "On purpose?"

Adrian filled his buddy in on his evening.

"That doesn't sound like progress on the professional front. That sounds like a date."

"It wasn't a date," Adrian said quickly.

"If you say so. I think you should let the job thing go, and cut your losses. There's no way she's coming to work for you."

"Come on, you know me better than that. I never throw in the towel."

"Oh, really? I got one word for you—Stacey."

Instantly, Adrian's smile disappeared. "That's different. She was a cross-dresser."

"Seriously? I thought you said she was crazy?"

"Don't get me wrong, she was a nut job, too—but she liked wearing men's clothes. She was wearing a suit when I met her."

"Good grief," Justin complained. "Where does your mother get these chicks from?"

"Trust me, I wish I knew. You'd think some of them wouldn't have issues."

"Didn't you say that very same thing about Milán not long ago? You called her crazy, too," Justin reminded him.

Adrian laughed. "Yes, but crazy in a sexy, hot-blooded Latina kind of way. Not with a straitjacket and Thorazine drips."

"See, I knew your interest was more than business related."

Before Justin could say more, Adrian's mother returned so he told Justin he would call him later and hung up.

Ushering her to the passenger side, he held the door while Norma Jean got in. When he slid behind the wheel, his mother eyed him with curiosity.

"You and Milán were very chummy."

"Well, we had ample time to talk to each other," he countered.

"Hmm."

Adrian secured his seat belt, started the car and then backed up. "What's the *hmm* about, Mom?"

"Nothing, sweetheart," his mother turned her head and peered out the window. "Nothing at all."

"Don't start. We just had a few conversations—that's all."

"Why are you getting so defensive? I just asked."

"Maybe because your 'just asking' tends to be the green light for you to start meddling," he pointed out.

"I'm sure I don't know what you mean."

"Mother, don't go looking for any patterns here. Milán and I simply discovered we had a few things in common."

"You mean besides real estate?"

"Yes."

"Amazing. So, when are you going to see her again?"

Adrian's grip tightened on the steering wheel. "I have no idea. We aren't dating, you know. If I run into her, great. If not, that's fine, too."

"But, I thought you were still interested in her working for you. Did you change your mind?"

"No, I haven't changed my mind, but I'm not about to pressure her. Look, let's play it by ear and we'll see what happens, okay?"

"Of course, darling," she replied sweetly. "I agree. You should see what happens."

Adrian turned to his mother. "Mom," he warned.

"Must you always be so suspicious? I simply meant it'd be great if you and Milán could grow to be friends and possibly coworkers, especially since you have so much in common."

When he visibly relaxed, Norma Jean smiled and resumed staring out her window. "Looks like you may need my help after all," she whispered.

"What did you say?" Adrian inquired.

"Oh, nothing, sweetheart," she said quickly. "Nothing at all."

Chapter 11

"Remind me to tell you again how much I hate these things," Milán groused.

Her neighbor, Tiffany Gentry, said, "Will you relax? I told you this was a good idea."

"My good idea involved a video store rental or Pay-Per-View movie, a batch of chocolate praline turtles and a comfy couch."

For a reason Milán couldn't quite put her finger on, she was in a pensive mood. When Tiffany had suggested that she get out of the house, she had resisted. Hoping that she had deterred her friend, she was surprised when seconds after they had hung up there was a knock on her front door. Milán trudged over and opened it, not the least surprised to see Tiffany on the other side. At five feet two inches tall, Milán towered over her neighbor, but what the shorter woman lacked in height she made up for in spunk.

Vivacious and shapely, Tiffany had dark brown skin, dimples and a high-wattage smile. She wore her hair short and spiked in a flattering haircut that never looked the same way twice. Milán had taken an instant liking to her from the moment she'd been juggling two moving boxes and Tiffany had jumped in to keep one from crashing to the ground. They were only two years apart in age and after several conversations, Milán discovered they had a great deal in common. In no time, her neighbor was her sounding board on everything and had filled the void left by her missing sisters. And just like Nyah and Elena, Tiffany never took no for an answer, either.

"Come on, girl. We're going out," she'd said pushing past her. "My boss hooked me up today with two tickets to see the Bulls game. I wasn't going to go, but after seeing you coming in a little while ago, I changed my mind. No more feeling sorry for yourself tonight. We've got an hour to make you presentable." Tiffany stood behind Milán and pushed her toward her bedroom. "No excuses."

Milán was about to protest, but caught herself. *Am I feeling sorry for myself?* She wondered if it were just because she'd been in town almost two months and she hadn't found a job yet, but somehow that didn't ring true. She admitted to feeling apprehensive about being unemployed, but it felt like more than that. *No, money isn't it,* she told herself. Without warning a thought drifted into her head. *Piñatas.*

As if on cue, her mother and her paternal grandmother drifted into her mind. Milán recalled her father's mother chuckling about the fact that her young granddaughter had never liked one of the staples of children's birthday parties: the piñata.

Whenever Nana Dixon commented on it, Pia would say it was because Milán never liked feeling out of control. The first time she was blindfolded and spun around was a disaster. At four years old, Milán did not scream, or cry. She simply removed the blindfold and adamantly announced it was someone else's turn. Her failure to continue in the childhood game had wreaked havoc with the birthday girl who had refused to speak to Milán after that. From that moment on, her family had called anything that caused real turmoil in Milán's life a piñata.

Milán wondered what the catalyst was for her manifesting that image. Deciding to ponder it later, she realized that Tiffany was right. It was time for her to get out and have some fun and that's just what Milán intended to do.

An hour later, Tiffany turned sideways in her chair. "Are you listening to me?" she complained.

Startled, Milán shifted in her seat. "I'm sorry, what did you say?"

"I said you seem bored. We're out and about, communing with nature and meeting new people. You should lighten up and let yourself enjoy the evening. Which, by the way, is much better than sitting home hugging a fluffy pillow and watching television."

Milán raised an eyebrow. "In whose opinion?"

"I'm just saying. You wanted to expand your horizons and that's what we're doing."

"By coming to see a basketball game?"

Tiffany was incredulous. "We're at the United Center watching the Chicago Bulls play the Miami Heat, aren't we? I thought you'd love seeing your home team. Besides, it's a great place to meet new guys, right? Take a look around." She nudged her. "This place is overflowing with them."

"I'm just not into basketball."

"Okay, but did you see the one that just walked by? It's a profusion of gorgeous men—in all flavors. I told you we'd hit the jackpot! All the testosterone in here is making my head spin," Tiffany cried with excitement.

Feeling a bit pinned in, Milán stood up. "I'm going to get some snacks."

Her friend nodded distractedly. "Want me to come with you?"

"No, thanks, I'm good." Milán excused herself past several people. After making it to the concession stand, she heaved a sigh of relief. The noise level was more bearable here than in her seat. Not that she didn't appreciate Tiffany's gesture, she really did. In truth, things were a bit dull as of late. She also missed her family terribly. That combined with not having found a job yet had surely made her apprehensive. *That would explain the piñata, right?* she asked herself.

Snap out of it, her inner voice chided. *You'll find something that fits you perfectly.* With some difficulty, Milán concentrated on the menu. Seconds later, a voice interrupted her in-depth contemplation.

"Do you always have this much trouble making up your mind?"

It was the third person that had complained about her taking so long to order. It annoyed her more than being indecisive did. Letting out an exasperated sigh, Milán didn't bother to turn around. "Look, sir, if it's such an inconvenience, go in front of me."

"If you insist," he replied stepping around. After a second he turned to face her.

Her eyes widened in shock. "Adrian. What are you doing here? Are you following me?"

He grinned. "Sorry to disappoint you, but it's been weeks since we've crossed paths. Hardly what I'd call a stalking."

"True," she countered with a laugh. "But don't you find it a huge coincidence that we're both at a major event like this—at the same time?"

Adrian shrugged. "Chalk it up to fate."

"I guess I'll have to." She watched him order his food. She used the time to figure out what she wanted. When it was her turn, she ordered a soda and popcorn.

He snickered when the man handed Milán her order. "All that time and that's all you got?"

"I'm not all that hungry, plus my friend would think I'm weird taking this long and coming back empty-handed."

"I'm sure he would," Adrian said, amicably.

"He is a she," she clarified. "Tiffany lives in my building."

"So where are you sitting?"

Adrian laughed when she told him where they were. "Thank goodness for monitors, or you'd never see the game."

"Very funny. Not like I'm watching it that much, anyway."

"Oh? Why is that?"

Because I'm sitting here trying to figure out what my problem is. "Uh, I'm just not that into sports."

Adrian turned left and then right. His expression held humor. "I see. Well, since you're in the middle of a sporting event that you don't care about, why not join a few buddies and me for dinner after the game? Tiffany is welcome, too, of course."

Milán was hesitant. "I don't know. I'll have to ask her."

"Great. Do you have your cell phone?"

When she nodded, Adrian gave her his number so they could meet up. After finalizing the plans, they both returned to their seats. Milán relayed Adrian's invitation to Tiffany and was hardly surprised that she had excitedly agreed.

"Absolutely," Tiffany had said when Milán returned and told her the news. "One of his friends might be single."

The general consensus was Italian, so they had picked Francesca's on Taylor in Little Italy. It was close to the United Center and a well-known Chicago gem. While they waited for their table, Milán took the opportunity to study her surroundings. The interior was casual, but she found it very classy. The rich woods paired with the colorful fixtures, black-and-white pictures and muted lighting gave Francesca's a relaxed atmosphere.

Luckily for Milán, she loved Italian and had no trouble ordering. After everyone ordered, the group started chatting.

During dinner, Adrian recapped the highlights from the game with his buddies. Pretty soon Tiffany jumped into the fray. Suddenly, Adrian turned and faced Milán.

"So basketball isn't your forte, right?"

"Not really," she admitted while munching on her seafood linguine.

"You see, that's odd. I would have pegged you for an avid fan," he replied before taking a bite of his pizza.

She stared at him. "Why?"

"I thought you would have enjoyed all the action."

"My father loves basketball so I've watched quite a few games in my time. I just never developed a passion for it."

"Now that definitely seems like something you have an abundance of—or was that temper?"

Color rose to her cheeks. "*¿Qué le dijiste?* What did you say?" she corrected.

"Just kidding," he held up his hands in front of him before dissolving into laughter. "You should've seen your face."

Realizing that he was only trying to bait her, Milán relaxed and continued her meal. "You're talking to me about tempers?"

she countered. "At least I didn't purposefully stand my date up to teach my mommy a lesson."

"Ha," he shot back. "Spoken like someone that hasn't been fixed up nearly enough by my mommy."

Their playful banter continued for some time before drifting back into the group conversation. A few minutes later, Milán's cell phone chimed.

She retrieved it from her pocket. "Excuse me," she said, getting up to answer it.

When she returned, she dropped it into her purse and sat down.

"That wouldn't by any chance be my mother confirming a hot date, would it?" Adrian joked.

"No, that was actually the hot date confirming for tomorrow," Milán told him. "Though how hot it will be remains to be seen."

That got Adrian's attention. He leaned in. "So who is this mystery man?"

"His name is Maxwell, and he's an accountant."

Adrian listened aptly while Milán described her potential date. When she'd finished, he casually leaned back in his chair. "Hmm."

"What does that mean?"

He shook his head while surveying her above his wineglass. "It won't last."

"And how would you know?" Milán scoffed. "I haven't even met him yet, and you probably won't at all, so what makes you the expert?"

Adrian tilted his stemware to and fro, the wine rolled along with his movements. When he spoke, his voice was calm, and filled with assurance. "I haven't gotten this far without listening to women's needs."

Milán was aghast. "I suppose all the women you've gone out with asked to be dumped, or stood up?"

"You hardly know me well enough to make such a broad statement," he shot back.

"Fair enough." She stared at him as intently as if she were

trying to figure out where the piece in a puzzle went. "So what do you like to do in your spare time?"

"You mean besides chase after women?" he replied in a curt tone.

Milán wasn't deterred by his remark. She simply waited for him to answer.

He sat back in his chair and folded his arms across his chest. "When I can, I volunteer for Habitat for Humanity and the company endorses the Chicago Coalition for the Homeless and several other charities."

"I'm impressed, Adrian. I think it's great that you're involved with the community—that you're willing to pay it forward."

He took a bite of his food. "Evidently. You were all ready to paint me with a broad brush, but our initial meeting is not usually how I operate."

"I'm seeing that." Milán was about to say more, but Adrian's eyes wandered past her, followed a young man across the room. Puzzled, she asked, "What are you doing?"

"You know, I think he might be your type," he told her.

She shifted in her seat so she could get a better look. She scoffed at his selection. "*¡Tu estás loco de la cabeza!*"

"*No estoy loco. No se apresure en despedirlo,*" Adrian said, seriously. "*él tiene algunas cosas a lo su favor. Un traje semicaro.*" He looked again. "Off-the-rack, I'd wager, but it'll suffice. *El es alto y guapo*—"

Milán snorted. "*¿Estamos viendo el mismo hombre?* Because I really doubt it."

"*Está bien, olvídate de lo alto,*" he laughed. "*¿Tal vez él tiene una gran conversación?*"

Suddenly, her mouth dropped open and she stared at Adrian in surprise. The color drained from her face. "Wait a minute. *¿Habla español? ¿Todo este tiempo has reconocido cada palabra que he dicho y no dijistes nada?*"

Adrian looked surprised, too. He hadn't realized they'd been switching back and forth between English and Spanish any more than she had. He looked slightly uncomfortable.

"*Sí, con fluidez.*"

"Why didn't you tell me that the day we met? You let me go on and on and you didn't even stop me," she whispered in an accusing tone. "*¿Cómo pudiste?*" Milán said standing up.

Everyone at the table turned toward them. Adrian took her by the hand and gently tugged until she sat back down.

"I'm sorry," he said seriously. "At first I didn't tell you because I was angry at you coming in and cursing me out, but—" he continued when she started to speak. "I realize you were completely warranted in your anger. I was wrong and made a huge mistake. Afterward, I wasn't sure if we'd ever cross paths again. I know it was childish and I apologize." He squeezed her hand. "*Perdóname.*"

Milán stared at him for several seconds. Adrian's gaze never left hers.

"*Si alguna vez me mientes una vez más...I'll clobber you.*"

"I won't lie to you again," he assured her. "Now do you forgive me?"

"Fine," she said. "But I'm still mad at you."

"Fair enough. Now, let's get back to our discussion." He tilted his head toward the man again. "He's perfect, right?"

She looked the man over and then turned back to Adrian. "I doubt it," she replied confidently. "He looked down as he walked by instead of straight ahead or around the room. A clear indication he's not sure of himself. Either that or he doesn't like to meet life head on," she noted. "Definitely not my type."

"Are you sure?" he pressed. "Maybe he's a diamond in the rough?"

"No, thanks. I'm a woman that likes my diamonds right out in the open where I can see them."

Adrian smirked at that. "Fair enough. Wait, I've got him. Over there to your right. The well-tanned man in the blue shirt."

"You mean the one with the laptop?"

"That's the one."

"You can't be serious."

"What's wrong with him?"

"He's stroking his laptop like it's a woman. Definitely a bad sign. His lady would be competing with his computer."

Adrian's expression turned mischievous. "And if that were you? How would you like to be stroked?"

A slow smile crept onto her face. "That would depend."

He leaned forward. His eyes took on a devilish gleam. "On what?"

"On who's doing the stroking."

Her last statement hung heavily in the air between them. The heat that breezed through Adrian took him by surprise. Milán cleared her throat. He watched as she reached for her water. He decided to focus on the ice cubes swirling around in her glass. That was a mistake.

Milán took a drink. Fascinated, he watched the condensation slide slowly down the outside of the glass. One ice cube disappeared into her mouth; he waited for it to reappear, but it never did.

Adrian watched her jaws clamp down to crush the ice between her teeth. She chewed several seconds before swallowing. He unconsciously swallowed, too.

Man, get it together, he chided. With as casual a smile as he could muster, he said, "Your turn."

"Okay." Milán scanned the restaurant in search of a potential date for him. Their table was in the corner so she was afforded the perfect vantage point. With a mask of concentration, she perused the diners. Suddenly, her face lit up. "What about her?"

Adrian looked baffled. "Who?"

Milán leaned in. "There's a woman at ten o'clock."

"My ten or your ten?"

"My ten, your two. I think she could be your type."

Taking his time, Adrian checked out the woman Milán pointed out. His eyes held humor when they hers again. "*¿Ahora, quién está loco en la cabeza?*"

Chapter 12

Milán didn't take offense at his accusation. Instead, it spurred her on. "Don't even sit here and say she's not your type."

"Oh, yeah, definitely my type, but she's on the prowl."

"Is that a bad thing?" Milán challenged. "She's gorgeous, well dressed and isn't wearing a wedding ring."

"*No va a funcionar.*"

"What do you mean it's not going to work? *¿Cómo puedes estar tan seguro?*" she continued.

"*Porque ella es depredadora.*"

"A predator?" Milán couldn't contain her snicker. "*Estás lleno de ti mismo.*"

"That much is true, but there's only room for one Alpha male in any relationship, Milán. We both can't drive," he said, pointedly.

"*Yo digo que estás equivocado.*"

Adrian's eyes glinted with purpose. "I'm not wrong. Watch and learn, lady."

Without warning, Adrian got up, moved his chair directly beside Milán and sat back down. If the rest of the group thought the action odd, no one bothered to comment. Now they both had a vantage view of the woman-in-question's table. He leaned his body closer to Milán so that they could converse without being overheard.

"*Mirala muy bien,*" Adrian commanded.

"*Yo soy,*" Milán said, quietly.

"No, really look carefully. You'll notice she's here without her girlfriends tonight. That's because they would give a man way too many options. Tonight, it's all about her. She wants to be the center of attention—without any distractions. It also ensures that any man thinking of taking a trip over to that table knows she's available." Adrian continued his observations. "You see how she's swirling her finger around the lip of her glass?"

Milán studied the woman. "Uh-huh."

"It's a seductive, hypnotizing move don't you think? Almost like a snake charmer."

Studying the movement, Milán's eyes never left the lady seated across the room. "I guess so."

"Notice how bored our femme fatale looks, too. Another green light for a guy because all he's thinking about is the things he could do to wipe that look off her face. Trust me, somewhere in this room a man is watching her like a hawk ready to pounce, but I'm betting he'll be the one getting pounced on."

As if on cue, a man got up and sauntered over to the femme's table. Milán sat transfixed as he stood towering over the woman. He leaned in to say something. It was several moments before she smiled with feline precision, and then nodded. A look of relief crossed his face and a millisecond later, it was gone. In its place was an expression of confidence. The man lowered his large body onto the seat across from her. Their eyes locked.

Milán was simply unable to keep herself from staring at them. It was as though she were watching a movie. The two people she observed moved as graceful as the slow stalking characteristics of a well-choreographed tango. One would make a bold move, the other would retreat. Seconds later, that person would take the lead, and the dance would begin again in perfect symmetry.

"No question on whether they're leaving together."

The deep timbre of Adrian's voice coaxed Milán from her reverie. She leaned farther back in her chair. Her eyes focused on his face. "How do you do that?"

A smile played at the corner of his lips. "What can I say? It's a gift."

"Is that what it's like for you?"

"Hardly. At least not with any of the dates my mother sets up," he replied drily. "Those tend to end a lot differently. Much less gazing and tons more explaining."

Milán noticed his face clouded over for a minute. She wondered if he was remembering Norma Jean's helpful hookups.

"Well, whatever it is," she said trying to lighten the mood, "I hope you never try it on me."

Adrian's eyebrow shot upward. "Is that a challenge?"

"*¿Cómo puedes estar tan seguro?*"

"Yes, Milán." His eyes glinted with amusement. "I most definitely think you just said it was a challenge."

"Dream on," she retorted.

The rest of the meal was spent in jovial conversation. Their experiment forgotten, Milán and Adrian joined in the rest of the table's conversation. After dinner, everyone congregated outside the restaurant for a moment before going their separate ways.

Adrian pulled Milán off to the side. "I'm glad you and your friend came to dinner."

"So am I," she replied. "It was really weird running into you in such a huge crowd. What are the odds?"

He smiled down at her. "Fate, remember?"

The way he looked at her made her skin tingle. "To fate then," she smiled. "Thanks again. That was a great restaurant."

"Yeah, I've been here a few times. You should put this on the short list if you're ever in the market for a place to go on your next blind date."

"You know, you're not as obnoxious as I originally thought."

Adrian chuckled. He leaned in and brushed a wayward strand of hair behind her ear. His fingers glided along her ear and cheek. "But you still think I'm trouble?"

Milán tried to pay attention to the conversation. It was difficult considering his fingers had just touched her skin. Alarm bells started pealing. *Focus.* "Of course," she teased, "but at least you aren't the obnoxious playboy I thought you were when we met."

A hearty laugh escaped him. "Thanks…I guess. So, does that mean you've decided to give my job offer serious consideration?"

She tilted her head to the side. "You know, Mr. Anderson, I think I might." Just then Tiffany joined them and asked Milán if she was ready to go.

Without warning, Adrian's hand closed around hers. "Good night, Miss Dixon. I think you've made a wise choice."

"I said I'd consider it," she clarified. "It's not a done deal." She shook his hand before lowering hers.

He flashed a broad grin. "I'll await your call."

Before Milán could say more, he moved off. The rest of the crowd waved goodbye and headed their separate ways.

"That was an awesome evening," Tiffany gushed. "I got invited out on a date," she said in an exuberant voice.

"Seriously?" Milán looked over at her friend. "That's fantastic, and I want all the details."

"I'll fill you in later, but first admit it. This evening was much better than a night on the couch."

Milán watched Adrian and his friends walk down the sidewalk. "Yes," she said, absentmindedly flexing her fingers. "I guess it was."

"Ooh," Tiffany said in a singsong voice. "You like him."

Milán stared at the ground in front of her. "Yes, I actually do. He's turned out to be funny, charming and I think we're developing a friendship. Weird, huh?"

"Not really, and no. That isn't what I meant and you know it. You *like* him," Tiffany said, pointedly. "Go ahead and try to deny it. Granted, I've never seen that doe-eyed look on your face before, but it's the same the whole world over when a woman finds a man that she's all gaga over. And right now…you are wearing it, *chica*…big time." Tiffany dissolved into a fit of laughter.

"I am not," Milán protested. "Besides, I've got a date tomorrow. It could be a very good one."

"You're right," Tiffany agreed. "It might."

Later that night, Milán sat cross-legged on her bed flipping through one of her favorite decor magazines. She rolled her neck in circles to stretch her tired muscles. When she opened her eyes again, her gaze caught the lightweight comforter folded neatly at the end of her bed. The large, bold stripes of white, orange and a cool green reminded her of eating cantaloupe and honeydew melons from a bowl on a hot summer day. It always made her smile.

Suddenly, she picked up the sketch pad and opened a box of colored pencils lying next to her. Milán would analyze a room and then give it a complete overhaul on paper based on her ideas. Her bed linens had given her a flash of inspiration. Soon the page was transformed into a fashionable recreation room that any tween girl would be elated to hang out in. It was an exercise that helped her relax, and after tonight she needed it.

When she had first reached home, Milán had showered, put on her pajamas and telephoned her parents. Over the next thirty minutes, she had conversed with her mom, dad and two sisters via two three-way conference calls. It was a hodgepodge of English and Spanish conversations going on simultaneously. To an outsider it might be viewed as a bit chaotic, but for her family it worked.

Now there was only the occasional whisper of a magazine page being turned or the sounds of her sketching. The lack of noise was deafening. Her hand poised on the paper as her thoughts drifted to her unexpected run-in.

Their evening together was not what she'd expected. Granted, he was still as cocky and arrogant as ever, but each time they crossed paths, Milán discovered a new layer. More traits surfaced allowing her to see him in a different light. Had he been right? Had she painted him with too broad a brush? *It's possible, but to agree to work for him? Is that really a wise idea considering you think he's hot?* she asked herself.

"Who are you kidding? You need a job and the bills aren't going to pay themselves." Her thoughts drifted to Eduardo. Her gullibility where he was concerned still left a bitter taste in her mouth. So did cleaning up his messes, but what was done, was done. Crying about it wasn't keeping her credit scores up.

With a loud sigh, she placed her things on the nightstand, got under the covers and stretched out. She placed her arms behind her head to get comfortable. Going over her options, Milán grudgingly admitted that only one opportunity had presented itself thus far. Was it worth holding out for another? Or was this the lifeline she was being thrown? If so, not seizing it would be an even bigger mistake than giving her heart to a consummate liar.

Suddenly, Tiffany's words replayed in her head. "You *like* him." Milán had flatly denied it the entire way home, but her friend simply wasn't buying it. The more she had told Tiffany she was imagining things, the more Tiffany countered that she was in denial. Finally, they agreed to disagree and Tiffany announced that she was a patient woman and had no problem waiting to see Milán eat her words.

With a loud sigh, she pushed her conversation with Tiffany aside. Business was business.

"I hope I don't regret this," she groaned aloud. Flinging the covers back, Milán leaned over to retrieve her cell phone from the nightstand. She scrolled through her contact list until she found the number. She pressed the screen and waited. When it was answered, Milán got right to the point.

"Okay, I've thought it over, and I accept your offer. I'll be by your office tomorrow to discuss it," she informed Adrian before disconnecting the line.

Chapter 13

Milán sat back in her chair and took a good look at the diagram she'd created on her computer. It had taken two hours, but she was finally content with the plan for her brand new client's Gold Coast condo. It had been two weeks since she'd accepted Adrian's job proposal. It had taken them a few iterations to hammer out her contract. The main sticking point was that she would only agree to work on a trial basis, and that she be allowed to take off for her upcoming vacation with her sisters.

"Where to?" he had inquired after she had told him about her annual trip.

"I'm not sure. That's the thing. Whoever's planning the trip surprises the others with the destination. We don't tell until we're almost ready to catch our flight, or cruise. All we can disclose is the climate so we know what to pack."

"Sounds like fun," he had replied.

Granted, he had been none too happy about the position being a trial, but in the end he had capitulated and she got her way.

Milán was surprised at how easily she'd transitioned into the office. Everyone had been extremely kind making it simple to get to know her new coworkers. Overall, Adrian was in tune with his staff, trusting everyone to their own areas of expertise. That lent itself to a very relaxed environment which she enjoyed, but the most unexpected occurrence was her newfound friendship with him.

Upon further exploration, Milán learned that she and Adrian

had a great deal in common—in addition to their repeatedly being fixed up by Norma Jean. She found it easy to open up about her past. Even her time with Eduardo and the pain his deceit had caused. Adrian had listened and offered his unique perspective when she'd asked his opinion. She smiled when recalling some of the conversations they'd had. Over the last few weeks, it had been facile for Milán learning his likes and dislikes. They'd spent a great deal of time together. Of course when the topic was about him, Milán discovered Adrian was almost an open book.

Since she'd come onboard, he'd done nothing to overstep his bounds. In truth, he was a perfect gentleman in every way. Still…there would occasionally be a look, or a jolt when they made physical contact that would plummet Milán into a sea of confusion. At those times, she'd remind herself about the line she'd sworn not to cross. Adrian Anderson was her boss and they were in a professional environment, and she would do well to remember that.

"There you are."

Caught daydreaming, Milán jumped. "Hi, Jeanie." Her hand came up to her chest. "You gave me a start. What brings you by?"

"I've come to take you out for a bite to eat. Sort of a con-gratulations-on-your-new-job lunch. I wanted to take you out on your first day, but things have been hectic for me lately. I've begun teaching a new senior water aerobics class at the com-munity center."

"Really? How exciting," Milán gushed. She glanced at the clock on her wall and frowned. She had indeed worked through lunch. "Jeanie, you don't have to take me out," she began, but Norma Jean was having none of it.

"Nonsense. We're going, and I'm not taking no for an answer."

"Okay," Milán agreed retrieving her purse from her one of her desk drawers. "I know when I've been overruled."

As they walked out, Milán informed the receptionist when she'd return.

Once they went out into the bright sunlight, Milán reached for her sunglasses and slid them into place.

"The receptionist is so serious all the time," Milán told Norma Jean as they began walking. "I've tried to get her to loosen up a bit, but she's like a rock."

"She's old-school, honey. She runs a tight ship, and isn't in love with my son. Two points sadly missing from her predecessor."

Milán digested that bit of information. "Good grief, is there any woman within a twelve-mile radius that isn't falling all over your son?"

Norma Jean linked her arm through Milán's. "Yes—you."

"That's true. I'm not interested in men that think women are nothing more than portable playthings. I was surrounded by them in Miami. You couldn't walk down the street without seeing one drive by with his fast car and jewelry-studded eye candy sitting next to him. That isn't what interests me. Not then, and certainly not now."

"My goodness, such conviction," Norma Jean observed. "You really think Adrian falls into that category? Especially now that you know him so well?"

"Don't you?" Milán countered.

"Oh, honey, he has his moments, but that isn't where his head's at these days."

"Yes, but being friends with someone is different than having a physical relationship with them. Personally, I think it's darn-near impossible for the proverbial zebra to change his stripes."

"Are you speaking from experience?"

"You could say that." Milán couldn't keep the tinge of regret out of her voice. "I thought my ex was reformed, but was dead wrong."

"Well, maybe he just wasn't the one you were destined to be with."

Milán was thoughtful. "I guess you're right."

Adrian's mother insisted on Milán picking the restaurant so she chose a nearby Thai restaurant farther down Halstead. After they were seated with menus, Norma Jean casually asked, "So tell me how your date went with the caterer?"

Milán made a face. "Hardly worth discussing. There was no chemistry there—at least not between us. Though I have to say his shrimp seviche was out of this world."

Norma Jean rolled her eyes. "You went out with one of the most eligible bachelors in the city, and the only thing you can provide feedback on is his food? What about the accountant you dated a few weeks ago?"

"He's a nice guy, but there wasn't any chemistry."

"That's too bad," Adrian's mother replied. "But back to the drawing board."

"Jeanie, I've got too much going on with work to be too concerned with dating," Milán said and then began to study her menu.

"Oh, please. Now you sound just like my workaholic son. You two really need to get out for a night on the town. I know the perfect—"

"No," Milán cried out. Blushing, she glanced up at Norma Jean. "I'm sorry," she said quickly. "What I meant was I've had enough blind dates for a while. No offense."

Norma Jean stifled a laugh. "None taken, dear."

Adrian was finishing up with a client when he received a telephone call. He let it go to voice mail. Later, while he was getting into his car he decided to check his messages. After deleting it, he checked his watch. "*Damn.*" He dialed Milán's number. After a few rings, he hung up and tried his office. When the line was answered, he asked to speak to Milán.

"I'm sorry, sir. Miss Dixon left not too long ago with your mother," the receptionist informed him.

"Do you know where they went?"

"No, but she did mention getting a bite to eat."

"Thanks." Adrian hung up and dialed his mother. He breathed a sigh of relief when she answered the phone.

"Hi, Mom."

"Hi, honey," Norma Jean replied. "What a nice surprise. Milán and I just sat down to eat. Why don't you join us?"

"I can't," Adrian explained. "I need to speak to Milán. It's important."

"Sure, hang on." Norma Jean handed the phone to Milán. "Hello?"

"Sorry to interrupt," he began. "I tried your cell, but you didn't answer. I need a favor and pretty darn quick."

Milán lit candles strategically placed around the first floor of Adrian's two-level brownstone. Located on North Dearborn Street in Chicago's highly desirable Gold Coast neighborhood, it was convenient to the Magnificent Mile and Oak Beach. Perfect for entertaining, Adrian's home boasted a small patio area in the front of the gated yard and a courtyard with a fire pit, seating and a water feature in the back.

An hour after his frantic phone call, Milán had transformed Adrian's first floor and outdoor area with fresh fragrant flowers and candles.

"Stop hovering," she chided seeing the anxious look on his face. "Everything is fine."

"Sorry, it's just that one of our newest clients is a big deal for Anderson," Adrian explained following closely behind her. "We've been trying to get the listing on my house for some time now. That she picked us to list her estate could open up lots of doors. She's very connected, and in this economy we need every advantage. That's why I'm...we're throwing this impromptu mixer. She'll be out of the country for a few weeks and I wanted to get it done before she left. I thought it would be good to extend the invitation to our other buyers and sellers we've acquired over the last few weeks, too."

"It's a great idea, Adrian. I'm glad I could help," Milán replied lighting the last candle.

Suddenly, Adrian was right behind her. He slid his arms around her waist and pulled her against him for a hug. "I'm glad you could, too. You're incredible," he whispered into her ear. "I'm sorry for coming between you and your date tonight, though."

Not realizing that she had closed her eyes, Milán opened them and eased out of his arms. She turned to face him. "Uh... no problem. He's fine with coming over here. I'm just glad we were able to get a small group together on such short notice."

Adrian snorted. "Free food and alcohol? Who could ever turn down such an enticing combination?"

As if to prove the point, his doorbell rang.

Milán ran her tongue over her teeth and smoothed her dress. She faced Adrian. "How do I look?"

His eyes roamed over her sleeveless wraparound silk dress. The vibrant yellow and orange material reminded him of a tequila sunrise. Milán's hair was swept up and piled loosely on top of her head. Her strappy gold sandals complemented her dress and the shimmering orange polish on her toenails. She looked amazing.

"Amazing," he repeated aloud. "It's like you've been kissed by summer."

She beamed at his compliment. "How poetic." Milán's hand swept through the air to encompass his black slacks with gray and black silk shirt. "You don't look so bad yourself—but then you knew that," she teased.

How long they stood staring at each other was anybody's guess. The room seemed to hum with a sudden undercurrent that reverberated between them. Adrian opened his mouth to say something, but the doorbell buzzed again.

Milán was the first to move. "That's probably the caterer." She said clearing her throat. "Don't worry, I'll get it." She hurried from the room.

Adrian turned to watch her leave. He could feel the tension they shared. That along with the way she had practically vaulted from the room told him that Milán had felt it, too. He had to admit that his life had been going along incident-free since Milán had started working for him. She'd done something no woman had yet accomplished. She had become his friend.

It had been a natural progression that he wasn't even aware

of. She was important to him now. Exploring more than a friend-ship would complicate matters. *Wouldn't it?*

Several positive things had resulted from Milán being in his life. The first was that their spending so much time together re-sulted in no dates-from-hell courtesy of his mother. The second and more important was that since Milán had come on board, Anderson Realty was experiencing a surge in interest for her staging services.

Adrian wasn't thrilled about her being there on a trial basis, but he'd have six weeks to convince her to stay on full-time. Not that he was worried about the caveat she had placed in her contract. He would win her over in the end. Adrian was very convincing when he needed to be, and thus far the only woman that remained immune to his persuasion, at the most inopportune times—besides his receptionist—was his beloved mother.

Adrian had to admit that the Love Broker had remained true to her word. His mother had not fixed him up with any women lately, and for that he was truly grateful.

In fact, Adrian had taken the reins himself and had secured his own date for the evening. A hot beauty named Aria that taught spin classes at his gym. She was tall, had black hair cropped short, a slamming body and a beautiful personality. They'd gone out a few times, and her being interested in casual dating had been an added bonus.

"Adrian, the caterer is here," Milán called from the other room.

"Thanks," he called out before giving himself a mental shake. *Get your head in the game,* he scolded himself before heading to the kitchen.

Chapter 14

The evening was a resounding success. Justin and Sabrina showed up, as did Tiffany, and most of Adrian's staff. His newest client arrived with her husband and a business associate, as did several other couples. Since the gathering was last-minute, Adrian had decided on a cocktail party. The caterer prepared delectable hors d'oeuvres along with a table filled with minidesserts. There was a bar set up, as well.

Introductions were made, and everyone broke off into smaller groups to converse. Milán was speaking with Tiffany, Sabrina and Justin when her date arrived.

"Excuse me, I'll be right back," she told them hurrying to meet him.

"Hi. Glad you could make it," she said when he came in.

"Me, too." He gave her a light hug and followed her into the party.

When she arrived at Adrian's side, she reached up to touch him on his shoulder. He turned around.

"Adrian, I'd like you to meet Stephan."

"Hey, how are you?" He shook the man's hand. "I'm glad you could make it."

Adrian introduced Aria to both of them.

"A pleasure meeting you," Aria told Milán. When she turned to Stephan, she stared at him. "You look familiar to me. Have we met before?"

"I don't think so, and believe me I would've definitely noticed."

Aria blushed as she laughed up at him. Milán glanced over at her date in surprise, but refrained from comment. The four of them parried a few topics until they were interrupted by Adrian's new client. Milán watched as he was pulled away to discuss business. She made an attempt to interject herself back into Aria and Stephan's conversation, but it was pointless. They were discussing the merits of almond milk over soy which was definitely not her forte. After a few seconds of trying to seem interested in health food, she excused herself and left.

She walked straight to the dessert table. Grabbing a plate, Milán piled a few sinful-looking delights onto her dish. When she bit into the first miniature cheesecake, Milán couldn't keep the look of euphoria off her face.

"If that's what you look like with food, I'd hate to see you with a man."

Milán opened her eyes to find Sabrina observing her.

"They say that some people use food as a substitute for sex." Tiffany chimed in when she reached Milán's side.

"I'm here to tell you both that I've joined those ranks," Milán confided sliding another spoonful into her mouth.

"Trust me, don't even think about it. All that depressing thoughts will do is cause you to add five pounds to your thighs, and no matter what people say, eating fat-free cheesecake is sacrilege. Honestly, if God would've wanted sweets to be healthy for you, would He have made them so sinfully delicious? I think not," Sabrina observed.

Milán eyed a miniature torte like it had a hundred dollar bill strapped to it. "You are seriously asking the wrong person right about now."

Tiffany popped a dessert into her mouth. "Honey, my fantasy is being immersed in warm liquid chocolate up to my neck and—"

"Ooh, those look delicious," Aria replied walking up to the table.

"They are. You should try a few." Milán reached over and grabbed a plate. She held it out to Aria.

"Oh, goodness no. I don't eat sugar. It's bad for your body. I love to look, and smell them, but this is my temple, you know? I've got to take care of it. Besides, I try to eat only organic foods if I can."

Milán. Tiffany and Sabrina exchanged glances. Milán was about to lower the plate on the table when Sabrina snatched it out of her hand.

"I'll take that." She started piling desserts onto it. Picking one up, Sabrina bit into it and beamed with pleasure. "Have mercy," she breathed.

"I see what you mean, Milán. Sheer decadence," Tiffany said loudly.

"Which reminds me," Aria interjected. "I'm planning my own little special evening with Adrian this weekend. I'm going to make a sumptuous meal for him. There's this recipe I've been dying to try out. Tofu with scallops sautéed in garlic and roasted seaweed—"

"You'll have to go to plan B," Milán interrupted. "Adrian doesn't like tofu, seaweed or scallops."

Aria frowned. "Oh, I see. There's always another one of my favorites, seared Ahi tuna with edamame." She smiled. "That's soybeans."

"Yes, I know." Milán returned the smile. "Unfortunately, Adrian doesn't care for those, either."

Tiffany and Sabrina exchanged amused glances.

Aria raised an eyebrow. "Oh. When he told me he was an avid health enthusiast, I just assumed that included diet."

"Not that I'm aware of, but then you'd have to speak with him about that."

"No problem." Aria glanced around. "So, is there any lighter fare here?"

"Uh, I don't think so," Milán replied. "This was thrown together last-minute and I don't think Adrian asked for any food alternatives."

Aria nodded and walked off without another word. All

three women watched her stride up to Adrian and wrap her arm around his.

"Now that was interesting," Sabrina commented. "She looked none too happy."

Milán agreed. "I'm sure they'll work it out."

Tiffany shook her head. "Why did she think Adrian was a health nut?"

"Who knows? The lightest thing I've ever seen him eat was salad, and that was loaded with chicken." Milán lowered her plate onto the table, but not before having one more treat. "Now let's go mingle."

Adrian was in the kitchen looking for another wine bottle opener when Aria came in. She came to his side. "There you are."

"Hey. Sorry I disappeared. The bartender needed another bottle opener."

"It's fine," she told him.

"So, are you enjoying yourself?" he asked.

"Not really."

Adrian stopped and glanced down at her. "I'm sorry to hear that. What's the problem?"

"Well, there's really nothing here that I can eat. You invited me to a party. I just assumed you'd have something by way of organic food here."

"Oh. I didn't know you had a special diet."

Aria stared at him. "Of course I have a special diet. I told you the first day we met, remember? You were eating a bag of chips at the gym, and I told you how bad they are for you. I must admit I was surprised to see you eating them considering how much of a health nut you are."

"Who told you that?" he scoffed. "Aria, I work out, but I'm not a fanatic about it."

She tensed. "I'm not a fanatic, either. I'm just very selective in what I put into my body. I assumed you were, too."

"Not really, no. Granted I don't smoke or anything, but—"

"You really shouldn't drink alcohol, either," she continued.

"Yeah, well that's not happening," he said and then laughed heartily.

Adrian stopped when he noticed her rigid expression. "Oh, you were serious?" He sat the opener down. "Look, Aria. Let me make it up to you," he said rubbing his hand on her shoulder. "How about we go out for a late dinner after the party?"

She shook her head. "It'll be way too late for me to eat. I've got a class in the morning, as well. I don't stay out late because it's important that I rest and stay hydrated."

"I see." He lowered his arm.

"I think it best if I left. To be honest, I really don't see how this is going to work out anyway."

Adrian was incredulous. "Just because I didn't have bean sprouts on the menu?"

"It's more than that," she said seriously. "You and I aren't really on the same page. I can't be with a man that doesn't view taking care of his body as seriously as I do."

"I'm sorry to hear that. Enjoy the rest of your evening, Aria. Would you like me to see you home?"

She stared at him a moment before she replied, "No thanks. I've got it. I hope you have a great evening, too."

Sometime later, Milán was talking to Sabrina, Justin and Stephan when Adrian came up behind them.

"There you are." He placed a hand at the small of her back. "I need you," he told Milán. "Our client has a few questions for you."

"Oh, sure. I'll be back shortly, guys." She hurried across the room.

"Seems like a pretty demanding client," Stephan observed.

"She is," Adrian conceded. "But that goes along with the territory."

"So, how long is this thing going to last? I've made plans to take Milán to a comedy show."

"Really? Who?" Sabrina asked.

When Stephan mentioned the name, Adrian shook his head. "That won't work, my man. Milán doesn't like him."

"Really? He's gotten great reviews."

"I know, but he's not her cup of tea."

"Hmm." Stephan was thoughtful. "I guess we can go see a movie. There's this new one I've been dying to see."

He told them the name, but this time Justin spoke up. "Actually, the four of us went to see that last week. It was great, by the way."

"Great," Stephan said sarcastically. "This evening is turning out to be one terrific date night."

"We're almost wrapped up here, and then Milán will be free the rest of the evening," Adrian assured him.

"Gee, thanks, that's awfully nice of you seeing that you're her boss and all."

"Not at all," Adrian replied, a smile playing at the corners of his mouth. He scanned the room. His eyes came in contact with Milán. When she glanced up, their eyes locked. She smiled at him and pointed to her watch. Adrian nodded. When he turned his attention back to his group, he saw Stephan's wary expression. "I'm sorry this has run longer than you anticipated."

"This wasn't exactly what I had in mind tonight," Stephan said in a tight voice.

Sabrina placed a hand on Adrian's arm. "You know, if Milán is going to get out of here any time soon, I think you should go help her out."

Adrian nodded. "I think you're right." His eyes met Stephan's again before he strode to the opposite side of the room.

Chapter 15

Their new client was holding court next to the fireplace in Adrian's living room. The deep tan walls, glossy white mantel with the black slate enclosure were the perfect backdrop for his client's cosmopolitan beauty.

Adrian stopped at Milán's side. "How's it going?" he asked in a quiet voice.

"Just great," she whispered back.

As Milán listened to the woman talk, she wondered if anyone else noticed how many times the woman said "me." From the enthralled look of her husband and business associate, and several of the other clients, Milán was guessing not. She studied Adrian as he interacted with the diva. He was at ease and never broke eye contact with her. He commented occasionally, but remained silent most of the time allowing her to do the bulk of the talking. It was almost like watching him size up the cougar that night at the restaurant.

Caught up, she studied his every move. When Adrian spoke, all eyes were on him. There was no denying the powerful presence he had. It wasn't something you could ignore. Thinking about his previous dating disasters, she almost felt sorry for the women if he had turned the magnetism up full blast. "They'd never stand a chance."

Suddenly, everyone turned to her.

"Who?" their new client asked with interest.

With horror, Milán realized she had spoken aloud. Her gaze

flew to Adrian. She thought he'd be angry to catch her not paying attention. To her astonishment, he was looking at her with amusement in his eyes. *Now that was unexpected,* she mused. Milán slapped a relaxed expression on her face and went with the first thing that popped into her head.

"My apologies, I was thinking about the special order I placed earlier this afternoon. One of my clients was insistent on getting a one-of-a-kind travertine chaise for her pool deck. Imagine it as an outdoor work of art that you could actually lounge on. She was convinced it would be a conversation piece with her friends."

The woman's eyes perked up. "Really? I'd think you'd be able to find them all over town," she said dismissively.

"Oh, not at all," Milán countered smoothly. "My designer lives on the West Coast. He flies out to fashion these furniture pieces around the owner's natural environment. He doesn't believe in working by pictures. He wants to see the outdoor space. It's all organic. To feel its essence—to be inspired by it."

There was an eager buzz among the people gathered around. The diva's eyes glazed over. Milán could almost see her mind racing ahead to the finished product. She exchanged glances with her husband. "Tell me, do you think he would design a piece for us?"

Milán refrained from answering right away. She tapped her index finger on her lower lip as if she were actually pondering the woman's request. "Well, there's no harm in asking, is there? I'd be happy to contact him…to check his availability."

"Fabulous." Acting as if it was a done deal, the woman slid her arm thru Adrian's and announced that they were leaving, but would expect a call from Milán when she'd commissioned their new artist.

Adrian glanced at Milán. They shared a private smile before he escorted his guests to the door. By the time he extricated himself, the rest of the party had moved out to the courtyard.

When he reached Justin and Sabrina, Adrian sat down next to them on a cushioned bench. He was all smiles as he relayed their good fortune to his friends.

"That's great," Sabrina enthused. "Congratulations."

"I owe it all to Milán," Adrian boasted when she came up to them. "She knocked it out of the park."

Milán's face reddened at his praise. Just then Tiffany came up behind her followed by Stephan.

"There you are."

"I'm just about ready to go." She smiled. "Sorry this took longer than expected. It went great with one of our clients, though."

"Will you excuse us?" Stephan said, guiding Milán to the other side of the room.

When they were alone, his smile faded. "You know this isn't exactly the date I signed up for."

His curt tone caused her to look up at him. "I'm sure it's not."

"So what's the deal between you and your boss?"

"Excuse me?"

"Do you always play hostess at his parties? That seems kind of strange, don't you think?"

Anger caused her eyes to brighten. "To whom?"

"Oh, come on. What man wants his lady to cater to another man?"

Milán gaped at him as though he'd lost his mind.

"First of all, Adrian is a friend and my colleague." she stressed. "Secondly, when did we decide that I'm your lady?"

"I guess we didn't. Kind of hard now, don't you think?"

"Quite frankly, Stephan, I don't care for your insinuations."

"I don't trust your boss," he sneered. "I guarantee that man has a hidden agenda where you're concerned. Call it a hunch."

"Well, I guess since you're a *man,* you would know," she said mockingly.

Stephan set his drink down hard on the counter. "I'm leaving now. Are you coming?"

Milán regarded him from head to toe. "No, I'm not. Enjoy your evening, Stephan."

He glared a moment before stalking off.

Milán watched him leave. She struggled to get her composure under control before she rejoined the others.

She ran into Sabrina first. She tried to look as cheerful as she could manage.

"Hi."

Sabrina frowned. "What's the matter?"

So much for composure. She groaned. "Nothing, just a difference of opinion."

"With Stephan?"

When Milán nodded, Sabrina guided her off to a more secluded section of the yard. "You want to talk about it? You look upset."

"Who's upset?" Justin asked coming up behind them.

"Shh," Sabrina told her husband. "I'm trying to find out what Stephan did."

"What did he do?" Tiffany said loudly as she joined the crowd.

By the time Adrian joined the group moments later, the mood was tense.

He turned to Milán. His eyes were penetrating. "Are you okay?"

She nodded. "I'm fine. I...handled it." She gave him a summary of her conversation with Stephan.

"What a rude bastard." Adrian's tone was glacial. "Lucky he left before I found out."

"If I'd known it would be such an issue, I wouldn't have asked him to come." Milán tried to keep the hurt out of her voice, but failed miserably.

"Don't you dare apologize for him," Adrian practically roared with anger. "His behavior was inexcusable."

"I'm not," Milán argued, her temper rising, as well. "I didn't appreciate him implying that something was going on between us just because I was here helping you."

"The guy's a jerk and good riddance," Tiffany huffed before turning to Milán. "Too bad he turned out to be such a jackass."

Trying to smile, Milán shrugged. "I'll live."

"Better to find out now before it got too serious," Sabrina reasoned.

Milán nodded. "That's true."

The Langleys said their goodbyes a short time later and

showed themselves out. As if on cue, the remaining crowd filed out behind them followed by Tiffany.

"Are you sure you'll be okay?" she asked Milán.

"Of course. I'm going to help Adrian tidy up and then head home. I'll call you tomorrow."

The two exchanged hugs before Tiffany left.

When they were alone, Adrian's arm went around Milán. He turned her to face him. "Hey, why don't you call it a night? The caterers did a great job of leaving everything tidy. I can tackle the rest by myself."

"Where's Aria?" she asked looking toward the house.

His expression changed. "Home getting her beauty sleep, I guess."

"Oh. Does she want a date do-over, too?"

"Doubt it. My body isn't enough of a temple for her so I doubt I'll be seeing her again." He shrugged. "Another one bites the dust," he joked.

They left the courtyard, headed up the brick stairs and into the house.

Milán watched him return furniture to the original locations. She moved to assist him.

"You don't have to help, I'm good."

"I know," she said kicking off her heels. "But I'm doing it anyway."

He shook his head. "Stubborn, aren't you?"

"Like you're just finding that out?" she laughed and grabbed the other side of his couch.

When the house was set right again they took a break. Grabbing some wine and snacks from the kitchen, Adrian poured them both a glass and then reclined on the sofa with his legs stretched out in front of him. "Well, that went well."

Milán sat sideways facing him. She swirled the dark red liquid in circles before she sipped it. "The cocktail party or our respective dates hightailing it outta here?"

"Take your pick."

"I think the business went well."

"It went more than well," Adrian corrected. "You were amazing, Milán. Just want we needed and the chaise longue thing? Brilliant." He raised his glass and toasted her.

"I think that's your fifth toast tonight," she laughed.

"Yeah? Who's counting?"

She brightened at his praise. "So what about the personal?"

His lips curled in distaste. "Hmm. Not so much."

Milán made a face. "You're right. That part of the evening was a bona fide disaster." With a sigh, she leaned her head back against the cushion. "What's wrong with us?"

Adrian grunted. "Can we help it if we don't like tofu?"

She burst out laughing. "Come on, clearly something is missing. How else would you explain it?" she reasoned. Standing, Milán started to pace. Her expression turned serious. "Maybe there's just something about the two of us that's…lacking."

"There is nothing lacking about me," Adrian snorted. "Or you. You've got some great qualities, Milán. You're funny, smart, gorgeous and real."

She stopped pacing. Her mouth dropped open. "You think I'm gorgeous?"

"Oh, please." He took a sip of his wine. "You know I do."

She pondered his words. "How would I know?"

"I told you, remember? The day we met."

"Oh, that," she dismissed. "That doesn't count. You were livid at Jeanie. You would have said the bearded lady at the circus was gorgeous just to prove a point."

He shook his head. "That's not true. My standards are extremely high. Hence me still being single, and my mother threatening to rent grandchildren."

Milán gasped. "She didn't."

"Oh, yeah," he told her. "And I distinctly recall telling you how beautiful you were. I didn't say that just because I was angry at my mother, Milán. I said it because it's true."

Her smile could have illuminated the room on its own. "You're wonderful, do you know that?"

He laughed. "Now that's definitely the wine talking."

"It isn't." She flopped down beside him. "Honestly, Adrian, I don't know how you date the women you do. You say your standards are high, but I beg to differ. None of them have substance, they're only concerned with the here and now, and they have no aspirations."

"Has it ever occurred to you that may be all I want?"

She shook her head. "It's not. You tell yourself that, but it's not true. I can see it in your eyes. It's merely camouflage. I've always thought you could do better, Adrian."

The smile disappeared. His eyes turned somber. "Of that I have no doubt, but then so could you."

"Me?"

"Yes, you. Since I've known you, you've had a steady stream of suitors, as well. Yet none of them has lasted past the third date. The question is why."

KIMANI
ROMANCE ™

An Important Message from the Publisher

Dear Reader,

Because you've chosen to read one of our fine novels, I'd like to say "thank you"! And, as a special way to say thank you, I'm offering to send you two more Kimani™ Romance novels and two surprise gifts— absolutely FREE! These books will keep it real with true-to-life African American characters that turn up the heat and sizzle with passion.

Please enjoy the free books and gifts with our compliments...

Glenda Howard
For Kimani Press™

Peel off Seal and
Place Inside...

W e'd like to send you two free books to introduce you to Kimani™ Romance books. These novels feature strong, sexy women, and African-American heroes that are charming, loving and true. Our authors fill each page with exceptional dialogue, exciting plot twists, and enough sizzling romance to keep you riveted until the very end!

KIMANI ROMANCE...LOVE'S ULTIMATE DESTINATION

Your two books have combined cover price of $13 in the U.S. or $14.50 in Canada, but are yours **FREE!**

We'll even send you two wonderful surprise gifts. You can't lose!

THE EDITOR'S "THANK YOU" FREE GIFTS INCLUDE:

Two Kimani™ Romance Novels
Two exciting surprise gifts

YES! I have placed my Editor's "thank you" Free Gifts seal in the space provided at right. Please send me 2 FREE Books, and my 2 FREE Mystery Gifts. I understand that I am under no obligation to purchase anything further, as explained on the back of this card.

PLACE FREE GIFTS SEAL HERE

168/368 XDL FV32

Please Print

FIRST NAME

LAST NAME

ADDRESS

APT.#   CITY

STATE/PROV.   ZIP/POSTAL CODE

Thank You!

✦ HARLEQUIN® READER SERVICE—Here's How It Works:

Accepting your 2 free books and 2 free gifts (gifts valued at approximately $10.00) places you under no obligation to buy anything. You may keep the books and gifts and return the shipping statement marked "cancel." If you do not cancel, about a month later we'll send you 4 additional books and bill you just $5.19 each in the U.S. or $5.49 each in Canada. That is a savings of at least 20% off the cover price. Shipping and handling is just 50¢ per book in the U.S. and 75¢ per book in Canada.* You may cancel at any time, but if you choose to continue, every month we'll send you 4 more books, which you may either purchase at the discount price or return to us and cancel your subscription.
*Terms and prices subject to change without notice. Prices do not include applicable taxes. Sales tax applicable in N.Y. Canadian residents will be charged applicable taxes. Offer not valid in Quebec. All orders subject to credit approval. Credit or debit balances in a customer's account(s) may be offset by any other outstanding balance owed by or to the customer. Offer available while quantities last. Books received may not be as shown. Please allow 4 to 6 weeks for delivery.

Chapter 16

Milán pondered his question. "*No lo se.*"

"I think you do." Adrian reached out and placed a finger under her chin. He tilted her face toward his. "What are *you* searching for?"

Milán couldn't look away. "*Yo…*" She stopped.

He leaned closer. "*Dimé le,* Lani."

She reared back so fast her wine almost sloshed over the side of her glass. "*¿Por qué me llamastes asi?*"

Adrian blinked. "*¿Qué?*"

"*Me llamastes Lani.*"

"So?"

"*Sólo mi familia me llama así,*" she persisted. "*Nunca antes esta me has llamado por mi apodo.*"

He shrugged. "Well perhaps I should have. I like it, it suits you." He studied her. "You don't mind, do you?"

"Um, no. No, it's fine. It just caught me off guard, that's all."

"Good. Now answer the question. What are you looking for?"

After a few moments of uncomfortable silence, Milán blew out a long breath. "I guess I'm looking for the dream like everyone else. A man that connects with me—on all levels, you know? Mental, physical and spiritual. I know that's cliché, but I've had less, and I don't want to settle for that anymore."

When he remained silent she turned away. "You probably think that's naive, don't you?"

Milán wasn't prepared for the hand she felt on her arm, nor

the expression on Adrian's face when their eyes finally connected. "I don't think you're naive." His hand moved up and down in a soothing gesture. *"De hecho, creo que eres bastante espectacular."*

Without warning, tears brimmed in her eyes. *Why in the world was she crying?* she asked herself. *Probably because he just called you spectacular,* her inner voice replied.

Adrian used his thumb to wipe the tears away from her cheeks.

"I'm sorry. I don't know why I'm crying. It's probably the wine. Too much and I get all emotional." She tried to laugh, but it got caught in her throat. She leaned over and sat her glass on the coffee table. Before she could react, she was being pulled into his arms.

He hugged her tightly to him. Milán clung to him. She inhaled his scent, a mix of the woodsy cologne he wore, the wine they were drinking and Adrian himself. It was a heady combination.

"Why are you hugging me?" she sniffed.

"Because you need one, now stop fighting and let me do what I want."

She smiled at his high-handedness. Somehow, it felt comforting to be held by him.

"I remember making you a promise," he whispered in her ear before releasing her, "that I'm having a damned hard time keeping."

Confusion crossed her face. "I don't understand."

The same thumb that wiped her tears moments before now wreaked havoc with her bottom lip. "Don't you remember? I promised you that I would not kiss you—without your permission."

"Actually, that's not quite true," she breathed. "I told you if you ever put any part of your anatomy on me again without my permission, I would cut it off."

His eyes glinted with a mixture of humor and something much more dangerous. "Uh-oh. It appears I've already stepped over my boundaries." He moved even closer. "The question is… do you want me to stop?"

A few months ago, Milán would have strung him up for touching her this way again. Now, a jumble of emotions rushed over her, and none of them felt safe. Did she want him to stop? Stop what? She wasn't exactly sure yet what it was they were doing, not to mention where it was going.

"Milán?" His eyes implored her with unspoken words.

"Yes," she choked out.

Adrian ran his hand from her arm along her waist and to her back. "Yes, what?"

Her heart raced and her mouth suddenly turned to desert. *Yes, I give you permission to touch me. Anywhere and everywhere,* her body screamed out.

Before she could utter another word, his cell phone rang.

Adrian swore under his breath before reaching into his pocket. He looked at the number. "Damn, I'm sorry," he apologized. "Give me just a sec."

"Can't you let it go to voice mail?" Milán inquired.

"I have to take this." He kissed the bridge of her nose. "It won't take long."

When Adrian moved away, Milán had to concentrate to keep from collapsing to the floor.

"Hello? Hey, how are you?"

Milán sat on the couch and waited for him to finish his call. Though she didn't mean to eavesdrop, it was hard not to.

"Sure. No, it's not a problem. I'm not busy so now is a good time."

He laughed. Milán frowned.

"Hey, you know I always have time for you."

Anger surged through her. *Just who was "you" anyway?* she asked herself. Milán bolted off the couch and sailed past him. So she meant so little that he could pretend that she wasn't even there? She stormed into the kitchen. Her skin grew hot and her breathing quickened. She would've left, but Adrian was standing between her and the door. There was no way she'd be able to walk past him without explaining what he did wrong and thus why she was leaving. Not that she owed him anything. Not after he'd just insulted her and they'd just…

"*Dios mio,*" she whispered, her hand coming up shakily to her lips. Mere minutes ago she had been more than ready to have him kiss her—and who knows what else.

It was clear now what a mistake that would've been. Here she was all hot and bothered, and he was trying to set up a booty call right in front of her. *Was it with Aria? Had she decided tofu didn't matter?*

Milán whirled around the kitchen needing something to do. It was spotless. A food enthusiast's dream stood before her: the Fisher & Paykel dishwasher hummed as it washed the party dishes; the commercial grade six-burner range was spotless, as were the granite countertops. Frustrated, she wrenched opened the French doors to his refrigerator and peered inside. She spotted a bottled water. Yanking it out, she opened it and downed the contents. She threw the container across the room and into the kitchen sink. The loud clank felt good to her frazzled nerves, but after about two seconds, she had to stride over and put it in the proper receptacle for recycling.

Sighing, Milán stood in the middle of Adrian's kitchen and stared. Turning three hundred and sixty degrees, she took in every nuance of the space. Striding over to the dark cherry cabinet below the sink, Milán bent down and grabbed several cleaning supplies, a sponge and paper towels. Taking a deep breath, she got to work.

Adrian ended the call with his mortgage specialist and turned his cell phone off before placing it back on the table. When his employee asked to go over some figures, he'd had no choice but to take the call. Taking care of business was the last thing on his mind right now, but it was important. He glanced around. *Where was Milán?* He'd seen her fly past him earlier, but had assumed she would return. They were about to tread into new territory, and Adrian was eager to pick up where they'd left off.

Just thinking about how good Milán felt in his arms caused his groin to constrict. He wanted her. Badly. Now he knew without any uncertainty that she wanted him, too. There was no way he could've mistaken her desire. It was as evident in her eyes as it felt in him. The moment she'd expelled a moan, Adrian knew her fiery passion would indeed match his own.

Now that he'd allowed himself to openly imagine making love to her, there was no way he could stop. Like a checklist, Adrian's conscience ticked off all the things he wanted to do with and to her. He imagined what her body would look like devoid of that delectable dress she was wearing. Her face materialized before him in the throes of desire. It was maddening.

He stifled a curse as his body reacted almost painfully to the images writhing about in his head. Standing, Adrian ran a not-so-steady hand over his face.

Milán was the most intriguing woman he'd ever met, and she had single-handedly done something no other woman had ever done: she had gotten under his skin. Wow. When had that happened?

"Milán?" Her name burst forth like a cannon shot. When she didn't answer, Adrian went looking for her.

He finally discovered her on her hands and knees in his kitchen. Her bottom was hoisted in the air and her head had disappeared into one of the cabinets on his island.

"*Lo siento, eso fue un trabajo… ¿Qué estás haciendo?*" he said loudly.

"*No mucho*," she called out.

Adrian arched an eyebrow at that. He took in his entire kitchen, and then regarded her again. His expression was incredulous. "Nothing? Milán, you've…completely rearranged my kitchen. I'd hardly call that nothing."

"It needed it," she said defensively backing out of the way she'd come.

Adrian's face took on an intense expression as he watched her rear end rock to and fro as she moved. Milán stood up and smoothed her dress. The material strained across her breasts for a few long seconds. Adrian had to force his eyes not to stare at their progress.

"The feng shui was completely off. The energy was all wrong, and it didn't make sense from a utilization standpoint. Now it does."

"Uh…it's not that I'm complaining, but it's just that…you rearranged my kitchen."

"It's fine," she said bending down to retrieve the sponge and cleaner. She placed them back in a utility bucket under his sink. "Here, let me show you."

Milán gave him a brief overview of the changes she'd made. Adrian stood in the middle of the room completely speechless.

When she opened his refrigerator, Adrian ran a hand over his face. "¿Milán, *lo que está mal?*"

She shut the door and looked up at him. "What do you mean, what's wrong? You don't like it?"

"I'm not talking about the kitchen," he dismissed. "*La cocina está bien. Perfect de hecho. Estoy hablando de usted.*"

"I'm good, but it's getting late. I really should be going," she turned to leave, but he blocked her path.

"Milán, you cleaned a kitchen that didn't need it—in your good dress. You organized all the food in my fridge by food groups, the water bottles are now all stacked and arranged by brands, and from the smell of it, you can eat off my floor," he joked.

When she didn't smile, he tilted her face up to meet his. "I'd like to think that I'm pretty observant, especially when it comes to people I care about. So tell me. What's upset you?"

"I'm fine."

When she didn't elaborate, recognition dawned. "Is this about my phone call? If so, I can explain. It was—"

"It's okay, no explanation needed. I'm sorry, I really have to go," she said backing out of the room. "Good night, Adrian. The party was great."

He followed her down the hallway and back into his living room. He watched in silence as Milán retrieved her shoes, grabbed her purse from his hallway closet and then bolted out of his house like it was on fire. Not once did she look back, and not once did he try and stop her.

This time when Adrian swore it was out loud. The harsh sound ricocheted around him. He strode into the kitchen, yanked open the right side door and scanned over his newly organized fridge. He reached for an alphabetized beer and then opened a drawer to get a bottle opener. When he didn't find one, he opened another drawer, and another. On the third try he found one. Adrian returned to the couch and put his feet up. He took a long pull on his beer. The more he thought about what they could have been doing right now, the angrier he got. "It's amazing, Milán. You can feng shui the hell outta everyone else's stuff," he said loudly. "Too bad you can't do the same for your own personal life."

Chapter 17

The next day, Adrian decided to arrive at work earlier than usual. He knew Milán would already be there and he thought it best to clear the air before the office got busy. *What are you going to say?* he asked himself. Part of him was still pretty pissed off that she'd left without an explanation. It stung that Milán hadn't been honest with him about her feelings. His phone rang interrupting the inner musings. He leaned over to pick up the receiver. "Adrian Anderson."

"My, you sound like a bear this morning."

Adrian closed his eyes. "I didn't exactly get a lot of sleep. What's up, Mom?"

"Nothing much," Norma Jean replied. "I was just calling to see how your party went last night."

"It's seven in the morning, Mother. You couldn't have called later in the day to ask me that?"

"You know mothers. We always know when something is wrong with our babies. So what happened?"

He stared at the phone. "Mom, I just want you to know that this whole sixth sense thing is kinda creepy."

"Then stop making me have to use it and tell me what's wrong."

"Nothing I can't handle, okay?"

When his mother lapsed into silence, Adrian ran a hand over his eyes. "Fine. Milán and I had a disagreement, okay? Now do you mind if we discuss this later?"

"Okay, but you fix it, do you hear me? Milán is a wonderful girl and I won't have you upsetting her."

"Me upsetting her?" *This is priceless.* "Mom, has it occurred to you that maybe this issue we're having is her fault?"

"No."

Irritated, Adrian decided to end the call before he said something that would only get him in trouble. "I have to run, Mom. I love you and I'll talk to you later. Tell Dad I said hello."

"I will, but I meant what I said. Whatever the problem is, you'd better fix it fast. These things have a way of festering. Just the other day your father and I—"

"Mom?"

"Oh. Sorry, dear. I'll talk to you later."

After he hung up, Adrian decided to go see if Milán was in her office. Her door was shut so he tapped lightly.

"Come in," she called out.

Adrian opened the door and walked in. Milán was sitting at her round table with papers and magazines strewn all over it. She watched him advance across the carpeted floor.

"Good morning," she said in a tired voice.

Adrian noted the dark circles under her eyes. "It appears neither one of us slept that well last night."

"I guess not."

"Can we talk?"

She nodded her head and indicated the seat next to her.

Once he had sat down, Adrian sighed heavily. "Milán, I think we need to discuss what happened last night."

"You're right. I'm sorry I ran out like that."

"I'd like to think that we've gotten to know each other pretty well. I know what you like, what you don't like, what makes you happy and when something is bothering you. Last night at my house, there was definitely something bothering you. I got off the phone to find my entire kitchen had been remodeled."

"Reorganized," she automatically corrected.

He arched his eyebrow.

"I know. Honestly, I don't know what came over me."

"I do," Adrian said moving closer. "We've been spending a

lot of time together, and we're getting closer. It's natural we'd have feelings of jealousy when other people intrude on our time together."

"I'm not jealous," she said quickly scooting her chair away from him.

Adrian stopped her progress with his outstretched leg. He used his foot to slide the chair back where it was and hold it in place. Milán's expression turned mutinous.

"Then what had you in OCD mode last night?"

She looked indignant. "I wasn't being compulsive."

A smile played at the corner of his mouth. "Uh-huh."

"If anything I was pissed off."

"About what?"

"You called me *nothing*, Adrian. How the hell did you expect me to feel hearing that?"

His mouth dropped open. "Come again?"

Without warning, Milán broke into a rapid-fire conversation with herself in Spanish, her arms waving wildly around her.

"Whoa," Adrian said trying to get a word in edgewise. When that didn't happen, he sat back, crossed his arms and waited.

Eventually, Milán stopped and switched to English. "On the phone, you said you weren't busy. That you had plenty of time for whomever it was you were talking to. Like I wasn't even there."

This time when she pushed back on her chair he let her go. She got up, moved away from him.

"I mean so little to you that I'm invisible now? What gave you the idea I wouldn't mind you setting up a booty call right in front of me, Adrian? What planet do you live on where you think any woman would be okay with that?"

Adrian stood up. "Lani—"

She held up her hand. "*¡Alto! No me llamas Lani!*" This is not a Lani moment, Adrian. You disrespected me last night and it was uncalled for."

He held up his hands in surrender. "Milán," he said quietly. "*Necesito que lo me escuchen.* Contrary to what you may think, I would never, ever disrespect you that way. What puzzles me is why you'd automatically assume the worst of me? Granted, it hasn't been that long since we declared a truce and started working together, but you just flat-out thought I would play you? That tells me you don't trust me."

"Part of me doesn't," she admitted.

Adrian's jaw clenched. "Don't hold back, Milán, tell me how you really feel."

"I'm sorry, but I'm trying to be honest."

He let out a harsh sigh. He strode over to stand in front of her, putting his hand on her back, testing her mood. "There are two things you need to know. First, I was speaking to a woman on the phone last night, and you're right, I did make it seem like I was alone, but if you recall, I told you it was work that called me. I was talking to our mortgage specialist. I didn't know how you'd feel about her knowing you were at my house at that hour, and what that could've implied. It just seemed easier not to disclose that bit of information. The second thing is that I need you to stop denying there's something between us that's more than just friendship."

She stared at him. She opened her mouth to speak, but nothing came out. Her eyes were wide pools of liquid amber. They implored him without words.

Adrian's hand moved from her back to her neck. Unlike the last time in his office, his touch was infinitely gentle. When his lips found hers, they were not there to punish or dominate. They were exploratory and tender.

She clasped her arms around his neck. Her fingers stroked his hair and neck.

"Milán," he breathed against her mouth. His hands roamed over her back. "This is about to pass that line friends don't cross."

Adrian buried his lips into her neck. She moaned in response.

"If you don't want this to go any further, you'll have to say so— *Ahora.*"

Talk? He actually wanted her to form enough words to make up a sentence? Was he crazy? Milán's body slowly moved toward autopilot. Desire left her weak and wanting nothing more than to find the nearest flat surface, hard or soft, to lie on so that they could take this exploration thing up another level.

It was harder to say no than Milán had ever imagined. She wanted Adrian with a fervor she'd never known. It was impossible to keep her body still. "Adrian," she pleaded moving against him.

His lips nibbled her ear. "*Lo dicen*," he commanded.

"*No puedo*," she croaked. "We're friends, and colleagues. That's where it should end."

"Tell me you don't want me and it will end here." He pulled away, but his hands still held her waist. "*Prometo*. I won't force you to do something you don't want, Lani."

She watched his lips move with a single-minded intensity. "I can't do an office fling, Adrian."

"I'm not asking you to, Milán."

"Then what are you asking? We should keep things strictly professional between us. It's never a good idea to date your boss."

His fingers touched her cheek. "I know, but we have a serious problem we need to address. You see, I realized after you left that I wanted to spend last night making love to you, not sitting on my couch watching late-night TV because I was too angry about your leaving to sleep."

Milán stared up at him for a few moments before she looked away. "I'm…sorry I misjudged you. I guess I was feeling a little overwhelmed by everything and just…panicked and—"

"Came up with any excuse so you could get the hell out of there," he finished for her.

She nodded.

"Aside from the damage that confession just did to my ego, why didn't you just talk to me? You have no problems letting me know what's on your mind any other time, and all the sudden you get tongue-tied?"

She looked sheepish. "That does seem rather silly, doesn't it?"

"Yes it does." He pulled her into his arms again. "I'm not going to pressure you," he said softly into her ear. "If you want to keep things the way they are, we will. I won't be happy about it," he teased, "but we will." Adrian tilted her face so that their eyes met. "Still, I can't deny that I want you, Milán. I know we work together, but we've got to figure something out."

"I know."

She knew Adrian was patiently waiting for her to decide if they should make love. *You're different. You are not one of the women that he'd kick to the curb after a week. He won't hurt you.* Since they'd become friends, they'd compared notes on their respective dates and he'd never mentioned doing anything that sounded ungentlemanly. *But would he tell you everything?* her inner voice warned.

Still, she couldn't run the risk of being hurt. She cared about him, a great deal, and if things did end badly, Milán didn't think it would be that easy for her to recover.

Her nerves were stretched taut. "Adrian, I think we should just…be friends," she blurted out. "Our working and personal relationship mean everything to me. I…I don't want us to ruin what we have."

Adrian searched her face. "Friends," he repeated slowly.

"Yes."

He lowered his arms to his side. "I see."

Milán watched him closely. He seemed to take her decision well, but she had a nagging feeling there was more to it.

That thought was driven home seconds later when he said, "Okay, but on one condition."

Milán stepped back. "What?"

"You go out on a date with me."

Her hand drifted to her chest. "*¿Es tu grave?*"

"*Soy muy serio.* You say there's nothing there, I say there is. I'm asking you out, Milán. If at the end of our date, you don't change your mind, I'll agree to your request."

"*¡Es una locura!*" she stammered out.

"It's not insane. I think it's the perfect solution to our predicament. You say you don't want us to become intimate. I say you do." Adrian placed a chaste kiss on her lips. "One of us is going to be wrong about this, sweetheart—and I definitely don't think it'll be me."

Chapter 18

Scheduled to meet Justin after work for drinks, Adrian was in a pensive mood as he stepped into HUB 51, a trendy hot spot in Chicago's River North neighborhood. It didn't take long for him to spot his friend. He strode over and sat down.

"Hey," he said.

"What's up?" Justin replied.

The waitress descended not even a minute later to ask him for his drink order. Adrian ordered a beer.

"Wait," he said as she turned to leave. "I already know what I want so we'll just order now."

They placed their dinner selections and handed the menus over.

"So how did the closing go?" Justin inquired after their server had left.

"Great."

"If that's the case, why do you look like you just had another run-in with Tony Ludlow?"

Adrian's lip curled in distaste. He paused before he answered. "Was it really necessary to bring up that guy's name?"

"I'm just saying, I usually only see that look when you've crossed swords with your arch nemesis."

"This is not about Ludlow," Adrian replied. "Granted, I did run into him at a business luncheon a week ago, but this is about Milán. I asked her to sleep with me."

Justin choked on his beer. "What?"

"You heard me."

"Dude, start from the beginning."

Adrian filled Justin in on his conversation with Milán, and their subsequent agreement to a date. While he listened, the smile on his face grew wider by the minute.

"You can't be serious."

"Extremely."

"You know you're my boy, but I have to admit. As far as the roadblocks you mentioned, I can see where she's coming from."

Adrian's expression darkened. "Thanks for having my back."

"I'm just saying, considering your lack of lasting relationships, it's not unrealistic to think she might be wondering what happens after that magic moment."

"I wish you'd stop watching therapy shows," Adrian quipped. "Either that or tell Sabrina to keep her opinions to herself."

Justin smirked. "You have to admit this is outta left field. Why now? I know you two are close, but you haven't said anything before about getting in to her—"

"Here we are." Their server reappeared with their food and Adrian's beer. They watched in silence as the woman set the plates down and told them to enjoy their meal. Conversation was momentarily forgotten as each attacked their dinner with gusto.

"To answer your question," Adrian said finally, between bites of his pulled chicken nacho appetizers. "I don't know. I just know I'm attracted to her, and what I'm feeling is a lot more than just friendly toward Milán. I'll admit I've denied it for some time, but it all came to a head at my house after the party."

Taking a bite of his green chili cheeseburger, Justin asked, "So what's next?"

"I haven't a clue. Besides, it's a bit early to start analyzing it to death."

"This is Milán we're talking about," Justin pointed out. "She's all about plans."

"Tell me about it," he muttered. Slicing his filet mignon, Adrian took a hefty bite. "Still, I want her to admit that she feels it, too."

"So you hatch some bizarre plot to win her over with one date? You really think that's going to work?"

Adrian grinned. "I'm very persuasive when I want to be."

"Don't we know it," Justin said wryly.

"Look, all I know is this status quo thing isn't working for me anymore. I need some time to convince Milán to at least give it…us a try."

"Maybe that's the problem. She could be worried it's business as usual for you."

Adrian dismissed that notion. "That's ridiculous. I didn't just meet her, and this isn't one of my mother's blind dates."

"I don't know… You've had quite a few one-nighters without Norma Jean's interference."

"Milán works for me, Justin. Do you really think I would have gratuitous sex with an employee?"

Justin put his burger down and stared at Adrian pointedly.

"Quit being an ass," Adrian griped, and then took another bite of his food.

Justin's laughter boomed above the din in the restaurant. "True, but you two work together. What happens if it doesn't work out? Then it's just awkward. Speaking of which, how are things with Norma Jean?"

"Quiet—and that scares me."

"It should," Justin agreed. "It's like the calm before a storm. It feels like any second she's going to do something *usual*."

"Justin, nothing my mother does could ever be considered *usual*. I was over for dinner the other night and she didn't grill me on my love life like she usually does—not once."

"Hmm. Maybe she's turning over a new leaf?"

"Well, whatever it is, I kind of like the new and improved Norma Jean."

"Still, it may not be wise to let your guard down," his friend warned. "The old one could be lurking around the corner. Have you told her about you and Milán?"

Adrian sat back in his chair. "No, and that's the way I'm going to keep it. No sense getting her in the middle of something that might not pan out the way I want."

Justin nodded. "That would just give her a license to jump in there and try to help you out. The Love Broker to the rescue," he laughed.

"Trust me, the less my mother knows about all this the better. In the meantime, I need to stay focused. Our date is this Friday."

"Friday? You're going to drag this out all week?"

"Yes," Adrian replied. "That's the plan. Maybe by then she'll be comfortable with the idea of us adding a physical component to the mix."

"Uh, good luck with that," Justin smiled as he signaled their waitress over.

"She wants me, I know it."

Justin rolled his eyes. "Of course she does. How could she not?"

A devilish expression lit up Adrian's face.

"Wait a minute," his friend said. "I know that look. What are you planning?"

Adrian crossed his arms over his chest. "I'm going to prove to Milán that we'd be good together."

"And just how do you propose to do that?"

A wide grin formed. "Easy. I'm going to turn up the heat."

Justin stifled a laugh. "Heaven help her."

"You did what? *¿Lo está loco!?*"

"Do you have to yell?" Milán complained.

Her sister laughed into the phone. "Yes, I do. You have lost your mind to agree to this madness, Lani."

"Nyah, it's just a date. I called you for an unbiased opinion, remember?"

"I'm your sister. Exactly how unbiased do you think I'm going to be? You say it's just a date, but then you admit that you want him. *Mami* is going to have a lot to say about this," her sister warned.

"*Sólo si le dices a ella, lo que le es mejor que no.*"

"*Oh, yo voy a decirle, estás jugando con el desastre.* What happens if you decide to date him and things don't work out?"

Milán ran a hand through her hair in exasperation. "You don't think I've thought of that? We work together. I know it would be all kinds of weird if it went pear-shaped."

"How long have you been pondering sleeping with him? I thought you said he has commitment issues?"

"He does…did…"

"Which is it?"

"I don't know… Maybe all the indecisiveness was just for Jeanie's benefit. He's always been the perfect gentleman with me. Well, after we got to know each other. *Antes de eso—*"

"*El era detestable,*" her sister supplied.

"Kind of. Besides, Adrian's only gone out on a few dates since I started working at Anderson, and none of them lasted very long."

"*Es evidente que una indicación de problemas de compromiso,*" Nyah pointed out.

"*¿No lo hago?* I haven't exactly had many follow-ups since Eduardo and I broke up. *¿Qué dice eso sobre mí?*"

"It says that you're being cautious—and rightly so. It also says that you haven't found the right man yet…*¿a menos que usted piensa que tiene?*"

Milán leaned back on her couch and tucked her legs under her. Her thoughts drifted to Adrian and the first and only kiss they had shared. It was explosive. There was no other way to explain it. Her stomach had felt like she was on a roller coaster when he'd pulled her into his arms and practically branded her with his mouth. Her body tightened further south just imagining what could've happened if he hadn't put a stop to it. *You know what would've happened,* her conscience piped in. *You would have melted like a box of chocolates under a heat lamp.* What would have transpired afterward made Milán cross-eyed with desire. *Heaven help me.*

"*¿Hola?* Milán? *¿Estás tu escuchando?*" Nyah practically shouted into the phone.

"Hmm? *Lo siento, estoy aquí.*"

"I'm sure I don't need to ask what you were thinking about."

"No, you don't. I can't help how I'm feeling, Nyah. Granted it's just a date, but I can't deny I might want something more."

"Milán—"

"*Tengo que ir.* I've got an early day tomorrow and I really need to get to bed."

"*¿Si usted lo dice, pero piensa en esto,* Lani? Once you cross that bridge, there's no turning back," her sister warned.

"*Lo sé. Buenos noches.*"

Milán hung up the phone and placed it on the coffee table. She lay there pondering what to do about the sudden predicament she found herself in. How did it get to this point so fast? One minute all was well, and they were enjoying each other as the best of friends. The next, everything gets blown sky-high with one kiss. Now she couldn't stop thinking about it—*or him.* Milán's gaze returned to her phone. She toyed with the idea of calling her baby sister, Elena. No. She wouldn't disturb her at this hour. Out of the three of them, she and Nyah were the more cautious. Elena flew by the seat of her pants in everything she did. If Milán asked for her advice, she would tell Milán to stop being a nun and drop the panties. She smiled because she could almost hear Elena's voice saying that exact thing.

"I've beat this horse dead for one night," she said aloud. Getting up, Milán went to take a shower. Unfortunately, the whole time she was in there, her thoughts centered on nothing else but the date she'd made with Adrian. Why in the world had she told him she just wanted to be friends?

"*Porque eres un cobarde,*" she murmured. Milán closed her eyes and tried to concentrate on anything and everything other than how she had felt in Adrian's arms. That good intention left the moment she rubbed the soap against her wet arm. From that moment on, lust took over. A lucid image of Adrian's hand moving down her wet skin manifested in her mind. It was enough for her body to react as though the image was real.

"How am I going to survive the next few days like this?" she choked out. Her body was pulled as taut as a violin string. With a loud sigh, Milán got out of the shower, grabbed a towel and began to dry off. *This is getting you nowhere. You work with him, remember? He's one of your best friends. You will not allow the possibility of sex to come between you and ruin this. Granted, it could be mind-blowing sex, but it doesn't matter.* "It's better this way," she said with conviction. Milán folded the towel and draped it back on the towel rack. She flicked the light off and padded into her bedroom.

She retrieved a pair of yellow boy shorts with a matching camisole from her pajama drawer, slipped them on and crawled into bed. Friday night loomed overhead like a blaring neon banner placed alongside an interstate. If she didn't get herself together, Milán feared she'd hop out of her clothes and beg him to take her the moment he walked through the door.

"*No puedo lo evitarlo.*" The words drifted out of her mouth like the soft flutter of a sigh. She rolled onto her back and admitted what she could no longer deny. "*Yo lo quiero.*"

Chapter 19

When Adrian walked through the door of his office Monday morning, he had one thing in mind: to drive Milán crazy. Unfortunately, his goal didn't go according to plan. He suffered one interruption after another, and by the time he got a chance to take a breather, it was after lunch and Milán had gone to see a client. *Great,* he griped to himself. How was he supposed to make her hot and bothered when she was nowhere to be found?

Since he had nothing scheduled that afternoon, Adrian decided to work the rest of the day from home. On the way out, he updated the board in the reception area listing everyone's schedule and left.

Milán moved a coffee table out of the way with a slight push. After she'd moved its counterpart, she took a step back and surveyed her handiwork. Staging rooms was one of the aspects of her job that she adored. Turning clients' personal spaces from pandemonium into crisp clean lines that made sense and fit their lifestyles, made her greet each day as one full of infinite possibilities. It also took her mind off her pending date with Adrian.

Her day was booked solid so she had yet to see him. If she were honest with herself, she'd admit to being torn about that fact. Part of her was trying to avoid him—and temptation. The other part truly missed seeing him.

"*¿Qué voy a hacer?*"

"Pardon me?"

Startled, Milán realized she'd spoken aloud and her client looked worried.

"Oh, I'm sorry. I was just talking to myself. I've so many fantastic ideas for this space I don't know where to start first." She smiled reassuringly.

The woman openly sighed with relief. After that last goof, all thoughts of Adrian were placed on hold and Milán got her head back in the game.

It was ten o'clock that evening by the time she finally made it home. Flinging off her shoes, Milán made a beeline for the bathroom. The next stop was the kitchen to grab the first thing she saw, a container of key lime pie yogurt. She got a spoon and bowl out of nearby cabinets and emptied the contents into the bowl. Next she pulled out a box of Cheerios. She dumped a mound of them on top of her yogurt and turned. "Dinner is served," she said before eating a spoonful.

Once she'd eaten, Milán put her dirty dish into the dishwasher. Dropping her discarded shoes off in the closet, she stripped and went to take a much-needed shower.

Later on the return trip to her bedroom, Milán heard her cell phone ringing. She ran into the bedroom to answer it. "Hello?" she said breathlessly.

"I'm not there, so what other reasons could you have to sound so breathless?"

Milán couldn't help the start of a huge grin. "You are so full of yourself."

"I'd much rather be full of you. In my arms, hands, my—"

Milán blushed instantly. Her breath momentarily suspended. "*Para eso*," she finally managed to croak.

"*¿Detener lo que?*"

"You know you shouldn't say things like that."

"*¿Por qué, te gusta?*"

Heck, yes, I like them. She sat down on her bed. "To be honest, I don't know how to take them, Adrian."

"*Que haces*," he said confidently.

"Is there another reason—other than you're trying to torture me—that you called?"

"That depends. Is it working?"

"*¿Qué pasa si me dijo que no?*" she shot back.

"I wouldn't believe you."

She was glad he couldn't see her smiling.

"So how was your day?" he inquired.

"Exhausting and completely satisfying at the same time." She sighed.

"I'll bet. Mine did not go according to plan, but I'm making up for it now."

Adrian filled Milán in on his day and bizarre run-in with a lady at the dry cleaners.

"You do seem to be a woman magnet, don't you?"

"There's only one I'm interested in attracting."

"For now," Milán scoffed. "You'll get bored of the chase soon and move on to another conquest."

"Is that what you think this is? Me filling the time between conquests?"

"*¿Se puede culparme? Tu no tienen exactamente el mejor récord de la pista, sabes.*"

To Milán's surprise, Adrian laughed. "That may be true, but I always know what I want. You should know that better than anyone."

Something in the tone of his voice gave her goose bumps. "Adrian, you expect me to believe that I know you better than anyone?"

"*Sí, que haces.*"

Those three words spoken with so much conviction warmed her heart.

"Milán, you should know by now that there is nothing commonplace about what we have. My track record may not be stellar by way of relationships, but that's because I've preferred it that way—up until I discovered that you weren't another setup and that I actually liked you."

There had been a question burning a hole in the pit of her stomach. Since they were baring souls, now seemed the perfect time to ask it. "When did you realize you wanted us to be… more than friends?"

"That's easy. The night you rearranged my kitchen because you were jealous."

Milán opened her mouth to protest, but she couldn't. He was dead right and there was no denying the motive behind his kitchen makeover. She *was* jealous.

"Nobody has ever done that for me before. I knew then that you cared—a lot."

Before Milán could reply her call-waiting beeped. She glanced down at the number. "*Es mi hermana.*"

"*Siguir adelante. Nos vemos en la oficina mañana.*"

"Okay." Milán hung up and switched over to her sister. "Hey, sis, how are you?"

"I'll be just fine when you tell me what's going on with your new friend with benefits, Adrian."

Nyah. Milán groaned inwardly. Nyah had filled Elena in on everything.

"What's this I hear about you deciding to sleep with him on Friday? I hope you plan on buying new lingerie."

"No, *no estoy comprando ropa interior nueva. Es a…la cena, no el sexo. Estamos a sólo platónica amigas,* Elena. *Nada más.*"

"Uh-huh. That's the answer you'd give *Mami* if she were on the phone, but she's not, and I know better than that. *He visto una foto del Señor Deliciouso. El está muy caliente,* Lani. If you aren't giving up the cookies to him, you damn well should be."

Milán couldn't contain the grin that ricocheted across her face. She wasn't going to inquire where her sister got a picture of Adrian, but Elena was right. It was getting harder to keep him at arm's length. Her granite facade was cracking, and soon it would snap completely in two. "*Tienes razón,* Elena," she finally admitted aloud. "I am tempting fate by going, but I don't care. It's high time I played with a little fire and see if it burns."

Chapter 20

Milán stood outside Adrian's apartment door. He'd asked her to meet him here at six o'clock for dinner. She glanced down at her watch. She was right on time. Taking a deep breath, she tried to squelch the nervousness and somersaults going on in her abdomen. *I am really going through with this.* "You bet I am," she said finally. "You're going to stop being a wimp. You wanted more, and here it is." Ending her spontaneous discussion, Milán pressed the buzzer on the door. Seconds later, it was swung open.

She almost sucked in her breath at the sight of him. Adrian stood in front of her in a dark navy apron looking altogether irresistible. She was dumbfounded.

"Hi," he said, then smiled before he leaned in and pecked her cheek. "Come in." He stepped aside allowing her to enter.

"Uh, hi," she replied following him into the foyer.

He closed the door. "I'm not exactly finished with dinner, sorry about that. I got a late start. Go make yourself at home."

"You're cooking?" Milán said with surprise. "I thought we were going out."

"Nope, I decided I'd wow you with my culinary skills for once." He winked.

What other skills can he wow you with? she asked herself.

"¡*Basta!*" she admonished herself.

"Stop what?"

Dismayed that she'd said it aloud, Milán blushed. "Oh. *Nada.*

Just telling my stomach to quit being so impatient. Mmm," she said sniffing the air. "*Cena huele delicioso.*"

Adrian slid his hand into hers. "Come on, Miss Dixon. I'm sure we can find something to tide you over till it's ready."

Milán trailed after him into the kitchen. He sat her down at a small table while he moved around the space. Milán was expecting to see chaos, but instead it barely looked as though he had prepared a meal. "You must really clean up as you go."

"I try not to leave a mess if I can help it. That way, if I'm tired after dinner, cleanup is no big deal."

"*Muy práctico,*" she replied, and then went to the sink to wash her hands. "*Puedo ayudar.*"

"How about you pick out the wine? We're having Ahi tuna, roasted baby potatoes and asparagus with a lemon dill sauce."

"*Por supuesto.*" Milán chose a bottle of pinot grigio and placed it in the ice bucket he gave her.

Adrian set a sampling of puffed pastries in front of her moments later. She inhaled the aroma.

"This smells delicious." She gazed at the food with avid interest.

"Dig in."

They conversed while Adrian finished preparing their meal.

When he started taking out serving dishes, Milán stood up. "Are you sure I can't help? I feel awful sitting here stuffing my face when you're working."

"*¿Quieres relajarte? Entra en la habitación de comedor. Me reuniré contigo en un minuto.*"

She gazed at him a second with uncertainty before doing as he asked. When she went into the dining room, Milán couldn't contain the smile teasing the corners of her mouth. The room was amazing. Adrian had candles lit on the fully decorated table, and others interspersed around the room. A pink and white lotus flower floated lazily in a water-filled crystal bowl.

Adrian entered with two covered dishes and placed them on the table.

"You outdid yourself," she complimented as he pulled out

the chair for her to sit down. *"Es muy bonito, Adrian. Gracias por la cena."*

"De nada." He sat the dishes down, uncorked the wine bottle and poured them both a glass before sitting across from her. *"Quería hacer algo especial para usted*, Lani."

Before she could stop herself, Milán leaned over and kissed him softly. Adrian responded in kind. His lips brushed over hers at an unhurried pace. His hand stroked her cheek.

When the kiss ended, they both were breathing heavier than normal.

"¿Qué fue eso?" he grinned.

"That was for cooking dinner—and something special."

"You haven't tasted it yet."

"I know, but you've never cooked for me before," Milán told him. "It's a big deal."

"Yeah? Well in that case, I made dessert, too. What does that get me?" He winked.

"That depends on how good it is," she shot back.

Taking a bite of food, Milán closed her eyes. "It's delicious," she said between bites.

"Glad you're enjoying it," Adrian replied. "So, have you found out where you're going on vacation?"

"Not yet, and we leave in two weeks. I'm so excited. I can't wait to spend time with my sisters and hang out. I haven't seen either of them since I moved here."

Adrian picked up on the throb in her voice. "You miss your family a lot, don't you?" he said softly.

Milán nodded. "Yes, I do. I've tried to speak to them as often as I can, but I really miss seeing them. We would get together for dinners, game night or shopping trips. Minus my dad, of course." She laughed. "He's not into shopping—at least not with my mother," she clarified.

He sat back in his chair. "I know the feeling."

"What about you? You told me you were heading out of town as well—business, right?"

"It's mostly business, but I'm adding some pleasure. An investor friend of mine has been trying to get me to look into an opportunity he has to renovate and purchase an existing resort in the Bahamas."

"That sounds exciting," she exclaimed.

"It could be a very good investment for me."

"Have you ever been to the Bahamas?"

"No. That's another reason why I don't mind mixing a little pleasure with business," he told her. "I could use a mini-vacation right about now."

Milán was about to comment when she turned her head and glanced across the room, and then back to Adrian. "*Eso la radio?*"

"*No. ¿Por qué?*"

"*Escucho música. ¿No?*"

Before he could answer, the sound grew louder.

"I know I'm not hearing things now," she said standing up. Milán walked into the living room and skidded to a halt. There in front of her were three men strumming guitars and a woman singing a soulful melody. Startled, Milán stood there dumbfounded. The beautiful woman walked up to her and presented her with one long-stemmed red rose.

Milán's fingers automatically closed around the stem. Unable to help herself, she lowered her head and sniffed the flower's heady aroma. When she finally glanced over her shoulder, it was to find Adrian observing her.

"*No sé qué decir,*" she admitted, her voice thick with emotion.

"You mentioned the mariachi band fiasco on one of your last dates." He sauntered up to her. Taking her hand, Adrian drew it to his lips for a kiss, and then spun her around and into his arms. They swayed in time to the music.

"So you thought you'd go one better, huh?" she inquired, her eyes shining with excitement.

"I definitely saw it as a challenge," he admitted twirling her around again. With his arms wrapped around her middle, Adrian held her in a close embrace. "*Así,* Lani." His voice had a seductive edge. "*¿Está funcionando?*"

Milán's skin tingled at the timbre of his voice. She closed her eyes and inhaled the intoxicating, incredibly masculine scent that was pure Adrian. Her toes wanted to curl. *Oh, yes, it was most definitely working!* The dinner, the music and his appeal were definitely making her "just friends" mandate hard to stick with. *That would never do.*

She opened her eyes and pulled away abruptly. "Wow, all of the sudden I'm starving. It must've been the dancing," she said cheerfully.

"Must have been," he replied with a knowing smile. "Let's go finish dinner."

Milán lowered her fork to her plate. "I don't think I could eat another bite. Everything was delicious."

"Thank you. My mother would be elated to hear your praise. She never misses an opportunity to mention that she taught me almost everything I know about cooking."

Milán's eyes widened. "I didn't know that."

"Then I'd say Norma Jean is seriously slipping. That's usually the first thing she tells anyone that'll listen."

"Are you sure she doesn't just tell that to your respective dates? If so, that explains why I wasn't let in on this best kept secret."

"Maybe, considering we didn't start off dating." Adrian's eyes held a glint of challenge. "That's not the case now though—is it."

"*No suena como una pregunta,*" Milán countered.

"It wasn't. Unless you're back to denying you want me?"

With a shake of her head, Milán got up and retrieved her dish. She went to grab Adrian's, but he batted her hand away. Standing, he picked up his plate. When she walked into the kitchen, he was right behind her.

She started loading the dishwasher. "It's not that I'm denying the obvious—"

"But what?" Adrian set his plate aside and pulled her closer. "What are you afraid of, Milán?"

She reared back. Her eyes held a hint of defiance. "*No tengo miedo.*"

The look Adrian gave her indicated he thought otherwise.

"You didn't ask me what was for dessert," he said changing the subject.

Her eyes twinkled with delight. "What?"

"Pound cake—your favorite."

"Don't tell me you bake, too?"

Adrian laughed. "I'm spectacular, but not when it comes to baking," he joked. "A friend of mine is a closet chef. He made it for me." He sauntered over to the refrigerator and removed a white cardboard box from the top shelf. "Could you grab the plates and knife I have on the counter?"

"Sure," she replied.

"*¡Venga conmigo!*"

Milán followed Adrian. "Where are we going?" she asked when he moved past the dining room table.

"Change of scenery."

She followed him to the courtyard and was again pleasantly surprised.

Adrian had practically engulfed the area in flowers. It had been transformed into a miniature garden paradise. Even the fountain had tea lights floating in the water on lily pads.

"Where did you find the time to set up all this?" Milán inquired.

"Anything can be accomplished with enough imagination."

"*Y el dinero,*" she added.

"That too," he replied, placing the box on the wrought iron table.

Milán set down the dessert plates and knife before Adrian held out her chair.

He sliced a piece of pound cake for her, and then sat down. He picked up a plump strawberry from a bowl inside the box. He held it inches from Milán's mouth, and when she leaned in and claimed a juicy tidbit of fruit, he grinned. Unable to help himself, he kissed her. The taste of lingering strawberry on her lips made him want more. His tongue slid into her mouth to duel with hers. The moan that escaped her lips was surpassed only by her bold move to repay him in kind.

Milán captured his bottom lip and nipped at it playfully with her teeth. At that point, Adrian was more than ready to knock the barrier his table had become onto its side and pull her into his arms. Instead, he lowered his lips to her neck giving a sensitive spot his full attention.

"Is there no end to what you're willing to do to wow me?" She shuddered.

"Sweetheart, I'm just getting started," he growled in her ear.

Chapter 21

Adrian was not sure how they did it, but somehow they managed to tear themselves away from the dessert interlude on the patio. After he paid the musicians, he convinced Milán to stay longer and watch a movie with him. She curled up on the couch with a bowl of microwave popcorn while Adrian placed a DVD in the player and turned on the television.

"So, what are we watching?" Milán asked between bites.

"You'll have to wait and see," he told her before he settled next to her on the sofa.

The black screen gave way to music and then a man sitting behind a desk in a newsroom announced that he had late breaking news.

Baffled, Milán stared at the screen.

"We have breaking news at this hour," the man began. "Sources tell us that Adrian Anderson has been planning to reveal his feelings for Milán Dixon for quite some time. There's no word yet on whether Miss Dixon reciprocates his feelings, but after all of the planning that went into tonight's date, we're hoping that we'll have some good news to report back to you soon. We will keep you updated on further developments as soon as we hear more. Now we return you to this evening's festivities."

Milán turned to Adrian. She opened her mouth to speak, but before she could, the anchor on the television began speaking again. This time in Spanish. He implored her to give Adrian a chance, and that he was a man that cared a great deal about her.

Enthralled, Milán sat glued to the screen as the man reiterated Adrian's commitment to her and his hopes that all would work out well between the two.

After that the screen went black. Milán set her bowl of popcorn down. She turned to Adrian and burst out laughing. "I can't believe you did that," she said in awe.

Uncertain of how to take that, Adrian shrugged. "I told you I was just getting started."

When Milán remained silent, Adrian tried not to appear bothered. Instead, he turned to face her. "Does that mean you didn't like it?"

"*¿Te gusta? No, no me gusta*," she told him flatly.

His smile faded. "Milán, look, I hope you didn't—"

Unable to help herself, she dove at him, wrapping her arms around his neck. She alternated between laughing, crying and hugging him. "I loved it," she sniffed.

Adrian let out an "umph" as he was propelled back against the couch by her exuberance. He closed his eyes and buried his head in her hair. "I'm glad."

Kissing his cheek, Milán let him pull her into his lap. "I can't believe you did that for me—all of it. Tonight has been so special, Adrian. Because of you."

He kissed the bridge of her nose. "You deserved it." He cupped her face with his free hand and brought his lips to hers. "I meant every word he said, Lani."

"Who was that?" she asked.

"A friend of mine. I called in a few favors." He grinned.

"*Dile que me encantó esta.*"

She tilted her head and kissed him. Seconds later, the kiss deepened. Adrian pivoted and leaned her back against the cushions. He traced patterns over her rib cage with his right hand. "What else should I tell him?" he said against her lips.

She ran a finger over his mouth and down his jaw line. "Tell him it worked."

Adrian's eyes raked over. "*¿Lo hizo?*"

"Yes. Did you even have a doubt?" she teased.

"You had me going for a moment. I was about to toss that thing out the window," he admitted. "I have one more question for you."

Milán's eyes glowed. "Yes?"

Adrian gave her the smile that never ceased to quicken her pulse. "Will you spend the night?"

She sat up slightly; a blush spread quickly across her face. "Wow, you really are formidable."

"Only when I really want something—or someone," he stressed.

"Adrian—"

"I'm not ready for tonight to end, Milán. Say you'll stay."

"I'm sure you could turn up the charm and I'd be agreeing in no time flat," she told him.

"That's true," he agreed. "But I want you to agree without me having to employ my...persuasion techniques."

"Really?" she said laughing. "And just how...extensive is this coercion of yours?"

Without another word Adrian rolled on top of her. He rained kisses down her neck and along her collarbone. With slow deliberation, he made it up to her mouth and tried his best to devour it. In less than six seconds, Milán's fingers were buried in his hair, and her leg was resting against his waist.

"Yes," she said in a raspy voice.

"Yes, what?" he demanded in a harsh whisper.

"Yes, you should patent some of these coercion techniques."

"So," he said with humor in his voice. "You finally admit that you want me."

"Yes," she said readily. "*Me quieres te*, Adrian."

Adrian's eyes burned with desire at her admission. "*Así que pasar la noche conmigo.*" He ran his thumb over her lips. "Because there's no way I'm letting you go home tonight."

Milán peered into his eyes. Their intensity must have tipped the scales because she immediately nodded. "Yes. I will spend the night, but," she added when a smug look crossed his face, "I'm not ready to sleep with you."

Seconds later, Adrian was roaring with laughter. He buried his head in the crook of her neck. "You're killing me."

"*Te vivir*," she smiled sweetly.

He stood up and pulled Milán quickly to her feet. A little too fast because she swayed against him.

"True enough," he chuckled, reaching out to steady her. "But I think it fair to warn you that I won't stop trying to get you to see things my way."

Milán got up on her tiptoes and kissed him. "I'd have been surprised if you did."

They did end up watching a movie and after it was over, Milán sleepily stood up and inquired about the sleeping arrangements.

"Follow me," Adrian replied taking her hand in his.

He doused the lights and together they made their way upstairs. Adrian ushered her down a hallway right off the master bedroom. She stood transfixed staring at the wall-to-wall drawers and cabinets. "You have a walk-in room?"

"More like a hallway," he dismissed.

"Whatever you call it, it's fabulous," she told him taking in the narrow, but efficient closet. Her hand moved reverently over the rich cherry wood. "All the times I've been here I can't believe I've never seen this."

"As much as you covet orderliness, I should've realized this would be your pièce de résistance of the whole house," he said drily.

Adrian stepped past her and opened a few drawers. "My wardrobe is at your disposal. Pick whatever you'd like."

Milán eyed several rows of neatly folded pajamas. She pulled out a wine-colored nightshirt and ignored the pants. "This will work."

"Great," Adrian replied closing the drawer behind her. He stepped inches closer to Milán until her back brushed up against the wall. "Now comes *my* pièce de résistance." He grinned lasciviously. His right hand rested lightly against her waist. "The sleeping arrangements."

Eyeing him warily, Milán held her ground. "Adrian—"

"What? Stop thinking the worst," he told her. "While it is true, I do want you in my bed, I'm willing to wait until you're ready. I was simply going to say that the guest room is down the hall and on the right. It's stocked with toiletries so help yourself. When you're done changing, come back into my room. I want to show you something."

Milán agreed. Adrian watched her leave his room. He sat on the bed and eventually leaned back. This wasn't exactly the way he had hoped the night would end, but it was a move in the right direction. He wasn't sure why Milán was so adamant that they not take their relationship to the next level. *What was she afraid of?* Granted, this was the longest Adrian had ever waited to consummate a sexual relationship—with anyone—under any circumstances. However, if Milán was still uneasy about making love with him, he would wait. "This relationship stuff is seriously going to kill me," he muttered.

Just then his cell phone rang. He retrieved it from his pocket. Looking at the number, he answered it. "What?"

"Is that any way to talk to your best friend?" Justin griped.

"I'm kind of busy right now," Adrian countered.

"How'd the date go?"

"We're still on it. As a matter of fact, you're interrupting."

"Am I?" Justin said eagerly. "You're in bed right now, aren't you?"

"Not exactly."

"Really? So tonight's the night? Man, I'd better let you go then. Call me in the morning and fill me in."

"Tonight isn't the night," Adrian explained. "Milán's spending the night, but it's completely platonic."

"What?" Justin bellowed into the phone. "I don't think I've ever heard you say that before."

"And you likely never will again," Adrian groused. "Not if I have my way about it. Look, I've got to go. Milán's going to be back any minute."

"Uh…right. I can't wait to hear about this tomorrow," Justin snickered before hanging up.

"That makes two of us," Adrian said before getting off the

bed and heading into the bathroom. He took a quick shower, brushed his teeth and put on a pair of dark blue silk pajama bottoms. Instead of the shirt, he opted for a matching robe. He doused the light in the bathroom and padded into his room. Turning out the overhead light, Adrian clicked on his nightstand lamp. Walking across the room, he cut on the floor lamp beside a chaise longue at the back of his room. It was positioned right in front of the French doors that allowed an uninterrupted view of the backyard.

"Hi," Milán said from behind him.

Adrian turned around to find Milán standing in the middle of his bedroom door. His pajama top rested midthigh giving him an expansive view of her long legs and bare feet. Her hair was damp and hung loosely about her shoulders. Her amber eyes looked darker in the dim lighting.

"Damn," he said aloud. "You really are trying to test my will-power tonight, aren't you?"

She smiled at his roundabout compliment and walked across the room. She stopped in front of him. "Mine too," she confessed.

Before he could respond, Milán moved past him to the open doors leading out to the balcony. She took in the white lights that were woven through the limbs of the trees in his backyard. The trickling sound of the water fountain made its way to her ear. "*Es maravilloso*," she breathed.

She turned to see him lying on his oversized chaise. Adrian held out his hand. "Come here. You have to get the full effect."

She padded over and placed her hand in his. He helped her settle in next to him. Side by side, the two sat silently listening to the water and enjoying the ambience.

"This is now my favorite part of your house," Milán murmured. Lazily, she stretched her body like a contented cat. "This is utterly relaxing. Do you do this often?"

"When I need to unwind," he said while gently sliding her hair through his fingertips. "Which is right about now."

Milán's hand rested on his chest. Her fingers moved past the opening in his robe to splay themselves against his skin. "I can't thank you enough for tonight, Adrian. This was the best first date I've ever had," she said solemnly.

He wrapped his fingers in her hair and tilted her head back. He stared into her eyes. "Me, too."

"Considering the horror stories I've heard, I believe it."

He laughed. The rumble of his chest did delightful things to Milán. "You know, there's more to it than that." He gave her a lingering kiss. "You wreak havoc on me in a way no other woman has before, Milán. Please, baby, let me show you just how much."

Chapter 22

Adrian's admission was a plea that burned its way straight through her core. It ignited something in the recesses of her body that threatened to engulf her in flames.

Something in his words and in his voice called to her on a purely primitive level. It made her slide up his body to wind herself around him like gift wrap. Adrian's reaction was instantaneous. Milán wondered if in fact she was offering herself up like a present and by the way he let out a groan of excitement, she knew he felt it, too.

His hands roamed her shoulders, down her back and then cupped her buttocks to hold her firmly against him. Milán felt the hard lines of his body and the full extent of his desire for her. It made her dizzy with need.

Milán sat up so that she straddled Adrian. Her eyes connected with his. "Adrian," she sighed. "You're making this harder for me."

His fingers grazed the four buttons keeping her nightshirt closed. "I'm supposed to. You know you want us to make love, Milán. Why fight it?"

Before she could answer, he pulled her down toward him. His lips brushed hers. Seconds later, he released her and got up. Milán's body temperature instantly cooled from the loss of his heat. She didn't like the feeling one bit.

He helped her up. "I think we need to say good-night—right now. Before all my good intentions go up in flames."

"There's only so much willpower you can muster in an evening, huh?" she replied.

"Something like that. I promised myself I would be the perfect gentleman. That's completely new territory for me, Milán. Normally I'm used to the evening ending a bit differently," he confessed.

"I don't doubt it. You think I'm a tease, don't you?"

"Hardly. I can understand your hesitation. I may not like it, but I understand."

He winked at her. With an arm wrapped around her waist, Adrian guided her to the door. They walked in silence down the hall to her bedroom. He opened the door and stepped aside.

"*Buenas noches*, Milán. I'm glad you decided to stay. *Dormir bien*."

"*Tú también*." She rose on her tiptoes and kissed him briefly on the lips.

Seconds later, Milán went in and closed the door behind her. She rested a hand on her stomach in an effort to quell the turmoil she felt. *How was it possible to miss him already?* she asked herself.

She glanced around the guest room. It was a warm, inviting room that rivaled a high-end hotel. The queen-sized bed was decorated with a comforter and matching pillows mixing colors of deep chocolate and ice blue. The dark brown wood headboard mirrored the two nightstands that flanked it. One had a silver candlestick lamp with a cream-colored shade, the other table a glass vase with fresh white lilies in it. The drapes were a variation of the bedding. A rich chocolate-colored chenille love seat with plush pillows sat regally in front of a wide window. The drapes were open and she was afforded a backyard view similar to Adrian's. He had impeccable taste and it showed in every room of his home.

Milán pulled back the covers on the bed and slid in. She picked up her cell phone. She'd missed two calls and three text messages. All from her family.

She read the messages and typed replies to her sisters' inquiries on where she was and why she wasn't answering her phone. It was rather late to call her mother so she'd put that off till morning.

A soft ding hummed through the air. Milán looked down and grinned. Elena wrote: Are you getting sexed up right now? If so, good! It's about time, y quiero detalles de la mañana!!"

No, I'm not having sex, and no, I'm not giving you details, Milán typed out. She laughed at her sister's dismissal of that vow and her warning to expect a three-way call in the morning. Seconds later, Nyah's text dinged into the silence with the same demand. Apparently, Elena had already filled her in. Milán bid both of her sisters good-night and turned off her phone. She flicked the light switch off and snuggled under the covers. Smiling, she stared at the ceiling for a few minutes before drifting off into a peaceful sleep.

Always an early riser, Adrian was up, dressed and on his way downstairs by seven o'clock. He noted Milán's closed door and decided not to wake her.

By the time his foot hit the last step, a delectable aroma invaded his nose. When he crossed the kitchen threshold, it was to find Milán bent over pulling a tray from the oven. He had a delightful view of her rear end and immediately said, "Now that is a wonderful way to start my Saturday morning."

Milán looked over her shoulder to see him lounging against the wall. "Good morning to you, too." She smiled. "Breakfast is almost ready."

Adrian sauntered over to her. After she sat the baking sheet onto the granite countertop, she closed the oven door. Adrian's arms snaked around her waist to turn her around. He leaned down and kissed her. "I thought you were still sleeping."

"Trust me, if it wasn't for my wanting to surprise you, I'd still be in bed."

"You taste like ripe strawberries."

She blushed. "Here," she said handing him a carafe. "It's such a lovely morning I thought we'd eat out on the patio again. If you don't mind?"

"Whatever my lady wants," Adrian replied taking the container.

Grinning like a schoolgirl, Milán grabbed a covered dish and headed after him.

They both made another trip back to the kitchen before finally sitting down.

He took in the Belgian waffles laden with fresh strawberries and powdered sugar and the ample helping of sausage on his plate. A wicked gleam lit up his face. "This looks almost as delectable as you do."

"How can you say that? I'm still wearing your shirt and my feet are bare."

"And you look sexy as hell," his said in an appreciative voice.

"You've outdone yourself," Adrian said after he'd devoured a mouthful of waffles. "I can't remember the last time I've had these."

She beamed under his praise. "I'm glad you like them. It's been a long time since I've had them, too. When I was…redecorating, I noticed you had a Belgian waffle iron. I've had a taste for them ever since."

They ate and chatted over their respective plans for the day. Adrian was going into the office for a few hours, and Milán had a client appointment later that afternoon and then shopping with Tiffany.

"Mom called before I went to bed last night and invited us over for dinner tonight. Are you free?"

"Of course," Milán said quickly. "Does she…did you tell her I was over?"

Adrian shook his head. "Did you want me to?"

Milán pondered that question for a few moments. Finally, she shrugged her shoulders. "I guess she'll have to find out sooner or later. She'll probably be wondering why I didn't mention liking her son. You know…like that."

"Ha. My mother is much more intuitive than we give her credit for—at least that's what she always says."

Milán couldn't help but laugh. "I believe it."

So you're ready to go public?" Adrian teased.

"Why not? Knowing Norma Jean, I bet she won't be the least surprised to find out we're dating."

"We're not dating," he corrected immediately. "There's nothing exploratory about this. "You're my girlfriend. End of story."

Her eyes widened and then a huge grin suffused her face with light. "Have you ever had one of those?"

Taking another bite of food, he pondered her question. "I believe I had one in the sixth grade. It didn't last, though. Mom kept trying to get me to buy her a 'friendship' ring. After that I broke it off. I didn't want her having any unrealistic expectations of marriage."

"Who, your mom or your twelve-year-old girlfriend?"

"Both," he said seriously.

Milán dissolved into a fit of laughter. Eventually, Adrian joined in.

"There is one thing we need to discuss," she said turning serious. "Since we're…together."

"Sure," Adrian replied leaning back in his chair.

"I've been thinking about branching out on my own," she said slowly. "Starting my own design business."

"I think that's a great idea, Milán, but why now?"

"I'm still in a state of transition so now's a perfect time and we're a couple. No offense, but I'm not too comfortable with office romances."

"Why? How many have you had?" he joked.

"Adrian…"

He reached over and took her hand. He kissed it. "I'm kidding, Lani. I understand completely and I'll help you any way I can."

Milán visibly relaxed. A brilliant smile spread over face. "*¿De verdad?*"

"*Claro.*"

She got up and plopped herself in his lap. She threw her arms around his neck and hugged him. "Thank you. You don't mind just being there if I need to pick your brain, do you? I want to do as much as I can on my own."

Adrian's lips grazed across her collarbone. "*Ahora somos un equipo. Lo que necesites, estoy aquí.*"

Her golden eyes brightened with tears. "*Eres el major.*"

Adrian rubbed his thumb under her eye. "Hey, you're pretty amazing, too," he said solemnly.

They spent the remainder of the morning just enjoying each other's company. Milán left when Adrian headed out to go to work. He walked her to her car, and then kissed her passionately before she got in.

"Thanks for last night—and this morning."

Milán chuckled. "You make it sound like we were…busy."

"That would have been great, too." Adrian opened her door and shut it after her. "I'll pick you up at five, okay?" He leaned down and kissed her again.

She started her car. "What should I bring?"

"A pair of sunglasses," he joked. "When my mother finds out we're a couple, her smile is going to eclipse the sun."

"*Yo lo creo,*" Milán agreed. "*¡Hasta luego!*"

Adrian waved as she pulled off. He took his front steps two at a time heading back into the house. He whistled as he bounded up the stairs and into his room. His phone rang so he stopped to answer it. "Hey, Justin," Adrian said after looking at Caller ID.

"Yeah, yeah, enough of the small talk," he quipped. "What happened last night?"

Chapter 23

As soon as Milán got home, she checked her voice mail messages. She wasn't surprised in the least to find several messages: two from Elena and Nyah, and one from her mother asking why she hadn't heard from her daughter lately. Milán looked at her clock and cringed. She just didn't have time for lengthy conversations with family at the moment. She decided to call them on the car ride over to her client's house. With a plan of action, Milán headed to her bedroom to shower and change clothes.

After bathing, she decided on a pair of gray dress slacks, a white sleeveless top with red pumps and silver jewelry. Milán pulled her hair up into a French twist. She flicked tendrils into place before brushing her teeth and applying makeup. Grabbing her portfolio and red handbag, she walked out the door and headed for her car.

Two hours later, Milán was sitting on Tiffany's couch with her bare feet tucked under her and a glass of iced tea in her hand. "I'm sorry I didn't feel up to shopping. My staging appointment ran longer than I expected. I gave her some homework to declutter so we could start staging the rooms, but when I got there it looked exactly like I'd seen it last week. Her open house is next Saturday so we have to be ready."

"You sure you don't want something stronger?" her friend inquired, pointing to her tea glass.

"This is fine. We're going to Adrian's mom's house. I don't want to show up tipsy." She laughed.

"Suit yourself. I can't believe the night you had," Tiffany said, dreamily. "What a romantic. Did you have a clue?"

"Of course not." Milán sighed. "I was floored…completely. There's was no way I could've imagined he'd go to such great lengths—"

Tiffany took a sip of her drink. "To bed you?"

A playful smile crossed Milán's face. "No. To surprise me. It's a night I'll never forget."

"I can tell by the blush," Tiffany teased.

"I'm not blushing," Milán protested, but touched her cheek with her right hand. "Enough about me, how was your date with Adrian's friend?"

"Fizzled," Tiffany exclaimed with a hand gesture. "There was no chemistry at all which was shocking considering the fun we had had after the basketball game. He's been moved to the friend aisle."

Milán set her drink on the table and turned to face Tiffany. "The friend aisle?"

"Girl, yes. He loves sports so that was a plus, but we're just not attracted to each other like that." Tiffany made a face. "It's like hanging out with my brother."

"You don't have a brother."

"Well if I did, it would've been just like it."

"Maybe you need to services of the Love Broker."

Tiffany scrunched up her nose. "Uh, thank you, but no. I don't need Adrian's mother fixing me up. Not with the horror stories you've told me. I have enough hit and misses without that kind of track record."

"Don't be so sure. She had great results with Sabrina and Justin. They even got married," Milán pointed out.

"Yeah, but she was trying for Adrian, wasn't she?"

Taking a sip of her drink, Milán said, "True, but it worked out in the end."

They chatted for a few more minutes before Milán announced she had to leave.

"I'll call you tomorrow," she promised Tiffany.

"Okay, but if something crazy happens, I want a call tonight."

Hugging her friend, Milán agreed and headed back to her apartment to get ready.

An hour later, Adrian was ringing her doorbell. When he took in Milán's sleeveless red lace dress and her hair in riotous curls about her shoulders, he nodded appreciatively.

"You look amazing."

Milán kissed him and replied, "You look pretty hot yourself."

In an instant, Milán was engulfed in his arms. Adrian's expression grew heated. "How about we skip dinner and stay here?" he said in caressing voice.

"We can't," she replied with considerable effort. "Your family's expecting us and I'm not about to keep Jeanie waiting."

Adrian groaned and released her. Reluctantly, he ushered Milán out her front door. "*Lo sé. Vamos.*"

Shortly after dinner, they were ensconced in a bear hug with Adrian's mother. "You two couldn't have made me any happier if you tried," Norma Jean confessed. "Well, there's one thing that—"

"Mom," Adrian warned.

"What?" she said innocently before releasing them. "I was just going to say that I'd love to have a picture of the two of you."

Her son looked skeptical. "You have a few already, don't you?"

"Yes, but those are all before you decided to get together. It's different now."

"They're still the same two people," her husband noted as they all gathered on the deck outside.

"Oh, Cliff, really. Get the camera, will you?"

Her husband shook his head and disappeared back into the house.

"I'm so glad you joined us for dinner, Milán."

"Thanks for having me, Jeanie."

"Oh, honey, you're welcome any time. I swear, I just can't believe the news," Norma Jean gushed. "Finally, the two of you are off the market. I never thought this day would come, and trust me I've been waiting for Lord-knows-how-long."

"The Lord and everyone else on earth know down to the second," Adrian said drily.

"Oh, don't spoil this for me, sweetheart. You know I love Milán like a daughter," she said grabbing both of their hands. She squeezed them tightly. "So, have you consummated your relationship yet?"

"What?" Adrian choked out.

"Have you had sex?" Norma Jean clarified.

Milán's face turned red and she placed a hand over her mouth.

"I understood the question. This is not a topic we're discussing," her son warned.

"Okay, okay. But you know it's perfectly natural—"

"Mother?"

"Here we are," Adrian's father announced coming back out onto the deck carrying his digital camera. "You two ready?"

"More than ready," Adrian said eyeing his mother with a not-so-subtle glare as he stood up and helped Milán to her feet. He wrapped an arm around her.

Heathcliffe glanced between his wife and son. "Do I even want to know?"

"No," everyone said quickly.

After a few pictures, Norma Jean ushered everyone back into the house for dessert. Adrian and Milán took the plates into the dining room while Norma Jean brought in the deep-dish apple pie and ice cream. They were all about to sit down when the doorbell rang.

"That will be Justin and Sabrina," Adrian said getting up from the table to let them in.

"Hey," he said opening the door. "Good to see you both."

"Hi, yourself," Sabrina said hugging him. She stood aside while Justin and Adrian patted each other on the shoulder.

They headed back into the dining room. When they entered, Norma Jean smiled warmly. "I'm so glad you two were able to join us for dessert. We've got such great news," she began. "Wait till you hear."

As soon as Justin and Sabrina were seated, Norma Jean filled them in.

Sabrina turned a shocked gaze to Milán. "I can't believe you two didn't say anything when we went out a few days ago."

"We just… Well it sort of happened recently," Milán confessed. "We haven't really had a chance to tell anyone, except Adrian's parents."

The next twenty minutes were spent in jovial conversation. Everyone caught each other up on the latest news. Adrian filled his family in on his upcoming vacation.

"That sounds exciting, dear. Milán, are you going?" Norma Jean asked.

"No, I'll be out of town, too. My sisters and I will be on vacation. We plan a new getaway every year."

"What a great idea. You know, Adrian. Your father and I aren't busy. We could go with you. It's been quite some time since we've gone Caribbean."

"Thanks, Mom, but I'll take a rain check," Adrian laughed.

Later, when Adrian was driving Milán back to her house, he asked, "Are you free tomorrow? If so, I'd like to take you someplace."

Milán glanced over at him. "*Seguro. ¿A dónde va?*"

"*No estoy diciendo. Es una sorpresa.*"

"That's not fair. You know I don't like surprises," she complained.

Adrian chuckled. "We both know that's not true. You'll just have to wait and see, *cariño.*"

The next day, Milán found out that the "someplace" that Adrian mentioned taking her to was actually many places. After picking her up, Adrian announced that they were going sightseeing. Milán was thrilled.

"I've had several places on my list of things to see, but I haven't quite made it yet," she told him.

"Good. Our first stop is Navy Pier."

Upon arrival they rode the fifteen-story Ferris wheel. While they were taking in a panoramic view of Chicago and Lake Michigan, Adrian filled Milán in on some of the history. "It's been a Chicago landmark since 1916," he informed her. "It was originally called Municipal Pier, and built for both shipping and entertainment purposes. It was renamed to Navy Pier to pay homage to the military branch after World War II. It was completely revamped in the 1990s to what you see now, one of the Midwest's number one tourist destinations."

"It's so beautiful," Milán enthused.

When they were back on the ground, Adrian guided her through a few of the shops, promenades and attractions. They stopped at Garrett Popcorn Shops to get what Adrian called a staple.

"It's the Chicago Mix," he said handing her the gallon tin. "It's CaramelCrisp and CheeseCorn."

"Isn't this too much?" Milán asked as they headed out of the store.

He popped the top and said with authority, "You won't think so after you taste it."

He was right. Milán took a mouthful of the yummy mix and declared herself a believer.

"This is the only way I want my popcorn now," she said between bites.

When she saw the Smith Museum of Stained Glass Windows, she stopped in her tracks. Seeing the look on Milán's face, Adrian smiled and nudged her inside.

They walked through galleries that housed over one hundred and fifty secular and religious-themed windows.

Next Adrian took Milán to see the historic Buckingham fountain in Grant Park. While she was marveling at the architecture, Adrian glanced at his watch.

"We've got a few minutes before the show."

"What show?" she inquired.

He placed an arm around her waist and whispered into her ear, "Wait for it."

The crowd began to cheer when a water show began. Milán

laughed and clapped right along with the other people as the center jet shot water way up in the air.

"It lasts for twenty minutes and happens every hour on the hour," Adrian informed her. "I'll bring you back one day at night. Then the water display is accompanied with music and lights."

"*Ahora dónde?*" she asked when the show was over.

"*¿Tienes hambre?*"

"*Un poco*," she replied. "Can we see a few more places before we eat?"

Adrian took her to the Shedd Aquarium and the Art Institute before they decided to stop for lunch at Lou Malnati's Gold Coast location for deep-dish pizza.

They placed their order for a Malnati Chicago Classic and conversed about their day.

"I'm glad you took me sightseeing, Adrian. This has been such a fun day. By the time the night's over, I'll probably have gained five pounds," she groaned.

"Even if you did, you'd wear it in all the right places," he said, lasciviously.

They teased each other up until their pizza arrived. Milán took one look at it and said, "I hope they have doggie bags."

When dinner was over, they decided to call it a night since both had early morning meetings. It was quiet in the car on the ride back to Milán's loft. They listened to one of Adrian's favorite jazz stations while Milán gazed out the window at the scenery flashing by.

Adrian rested his right hand on Milán's left thigh. "*¿Dormido?*"

"*No, pero podría pronto.*"

He laughed. "You and me both."

When they reached her apartment, Adrian walked her to her door. When Milán opened the door and went in she turned around. "Would you like to come in?"

In a split second, Adrian had backed her up against her front door and was kissing her passionately. Milán wrapped her arms around his neck. One minute later, they parted.

"Yes, but probably not a good idea," he replied with slow deliberation.

"*Sí, no buena idea*," she said, breathlessly. "*Bueños noches*, Adrian. *Gracias por hoy.*"

He kissed her a final time and released her. "*Con mucho gusto.*"

Milán shut the door behind Adrian and locked it. She leaned against it for a moment and placed her hand on her chest. "*El es muy caliente.*"

Chapter 24

One week passed in complete chaos for Milán and Adrian. Both were swamped with work with little time to spend together outside the office. They were finally able to squeeze in a late dinner at a neighborhood restaurant near Adrian's house.

"I can't believe that we're both leaving tomorrow," Milán said, tiredly.

He swept a lock of hair behind her ear. "I know. It's been crazy lately. Not much time for extracurricular activities," he lamented.

"I miss you," she confessed.

"I miss you, too. I wish you were going with me."

"Not as much as I do," she joked. "I wish I could reschedule my trip."

"Your sisters would kill you."

"*Muertos*," she laughed. "I still don't know where we're going, but one thing is for sure, I'm definitely ready for a vacation. I'm exhausted."

"We'll both be back in a week, and we can make up for lost time then."

Milán entwined her fingers with Adrian's. "*¿Promesa?*"

He leaned in and kissed her. "*Prometo.*"

After their meal, they walked back to Adrian's house. When they got there, he said, "How about we both shower and meet up in my room?"

"Deal," she said heading up the stairs while he locked up.

Milán took a quick shower and put on a purple silk chemise with a matching robe that she'd left there in case of impromptu sleepovers. She went to Adrian's door and tapped lightly. His muffled voice bid her to enter.

"You know you don't have to knock," he told her. "Just come in."

She waved her hand in the direction of his bare chest and pajama bottoms. "What if you were in the middle of changing?"

The smoldering look he gave her could have ignited a candle. "I wouldn't mind in the least."

"Nor would I."

Adrian's head snapped up at her words. "*Eso es peligroso, cariño.*"

She bit her lower lip. "I know it's dangerous, but I find that I can't help myself when I'm with you."

Without warning, Adrian strode over and hauled Milán up against him. His lips closed over hers with an intensity he'd never shown before. Milán's knees almost buckled. He released her arms and she immediately grasped his shoulders for support. Before she could utter a word, he picked her up and headed for the bed. He lowered her onto the thick mattress.

"Adrian," Milán choked out.

"There's no way we're not making love tonight." His eyes raked over her flushed face.

"No," she said quickly raising herself up on her elbows. "Our first time can't be the day before we both leave. That would be horrible."

"Why?" he demanded. "It's the perfect going away gift," he countered running his lips down the side of her neck.

"Please," she implored him. "Can't we wait a week? When we get back I promise we'll spend an entire weekend locked away here. It will be incredible," she assured him.

"It could be incredible now," he said thickly.

Milán kissed him before running a hand up his back. "*Yo se.*"

He stared down at her. "You're killing me."

"So you've said." She gazed up at him with an expectant look.

"Fine," he grumbled. "I can't believe I'm saying this, but we'll wait. One week, Milán. After that—"

She wrapped her arms around his neck and hugged him. "*Soy todo tuyo.*"

"Good." He grinned and unbelted her robe. He slid the material open with his right hand, and then ran it slowly down her stomach.

"*¿Qué estás haciendo?*" she asked suspiciously.

The smile he gave her was definitely carnal. "Giving you something to remember me by."

Milán returned the magazine to the seat pocket in front of her. There was no way she could concentrate on what she was reading. Not when her thoughts kept drifting back to her incredible night with Adrian. She closed her eyes. Luckily for her, the two passengers seated next to her were engrossed in a book and a laptop movie, respectively. Her flight to Miami would be just under three hours. That allowed her all sorts of time to recall some of the heart-stopping details from last night. Adrian had given her much more than just *something* to remember him by. He'd ignited a passion in her that refused to be doused.

Madre de misericordia. Adrian had rocked her with a desire that left her senseless. From the moment his hand slid down her body, Adrian hadn't stopped his fingers from tormenting her until she was shaking beneath him begging for release. And when it came, Milán practically saw stars. She'd writhed beneath him as wave after wave of pleasure ravaged her body. Once his fingers stilled, Adrian held Milán until her body stopped trembling and her breathing returned to normal.

Intent on returning the favor, she wasn't happy when Adrian told her that he would wait until they came home to finish what they'd started.

"Tonight is all about you, Lani," he'd told her.

Remembering his words, it was like her body was on a countdown until they were in each other's arms again. Until they consummated their love. That thought caused Milán to snap to attention. Her eyes wrenched open and her breath was shallow.

Their love? Did Adrian love her? More importantly, did she love him? How could she be certain of his affections? Everything was incredible between them, and had been for months. Now, they were even more simpatico, but…was it love? *¡Que dilemma!* She groaned inwardly. Deciding not to think everything to death, Milán tried to relax against her seat and will herself to fall asleep.

Hours later, her plane landed at Miami International Airport. Pulling her luggage behind her, she walked to their rendezvous point. When she saw her sister, she stepped up the pace. "Nyah," she cried stopping in front of her.

"¡Es muy bueno verte!" Her sister hugged her tightly. *"Te he echado."*

"I've missed you, too," Milán said excitedly.

Before either sister could speak, they were engulfed in Elena's embrace.

"What a family reunion." Elena laughed as the three of them hugged and kissed each other.

"I'm so glad to see both of you," Milán replied, her eyes full of tears. "It's been too long."

"That's what this trip is for," Elena said picking up a piece of Milán's luggage.

"Speaking of which," Milán said taking the other bag, "it's time to tell me where we're going."

"You're right." Nyah grinned and cast a conspiratorial glance at Elena. "The Caribbean awaits, Lani. We are heading to the Bahamas!"

Chapter 25

Adrian had been in the Bahamas for four days and was ready to leave. It was not that the white sandy beaches were unappealing, or the idyllic views not breathtaking enough. The problem was thoughts of Milán kept invading his business, and his peace of mind. Delectable remnants of their last night together caused his body to react at the most inopportune times. He had sent her a few playful text messages to entertain himself but also to let her know she was on his mind.

"Adrian, are you listening to me?" Tomás Moreno said loudly.

"Hmm? Oh, sorry." Adrian ran a hand over his face.

"Is something wrong? I know the last place wasn't all that great, but we have several more to look over before we head back to Nassau."

"It's true, I thought the property too small, and the landscaping wasn't that appealing either, but that isn't the issue. I just have a few things on my mind." Adrian took a deep breath. "So what's next?"

"Next," his buddy said eagerly, "we check out an eco-friendly hotel that just came on the market, and then we're heading to the Harbour Lobster and Fish Company in Port Lucaya for lunch. I thought we'd go Cajun today."

"Sounds good," Adrian said trying to sound enthusiastic. "I'm ready."

"Milán, are you ready?"

"In a minute," she called from the bathroom. "I'm just putting sunscreen on."

"How much body do you have left?" Elena complained. "You've been in there twenty minutes."

"You're on vacation, remember?" Milán reasoned. "Why in the world would you be clock-watching? Relax."

"She's never been good at that," Nyah chimed in. She reached for her camera. "You two meet me outside. I'm going to be by the pool doing some people watching."

"You mean man watching," Milán called out.

"Well of course. Vacation, right? If I don't engage in some hot, torrid fling while I'm here, what's the point?"

"You need to find one for Milán while you're at it," Elena joked. "She's strung tighter than a bow."

"Not interested." Milán came back into the room and grabbed her beach bag off the bed.

Nyah made a face. "Oh right, you're saving yourself for Mr. Wonderful."

"Saving herself?" Elena spun around to stare at her Nyah. "She didn't take my advice and drop the panties?"

"Oh she dropped them, all right," Nyah joked. "She just didn't keep them down."

"Hey," Milán interrupted. "Am I not standing right here?"

"You stand right there. I'm going to find myself a date for this evening," Nyah boldly proclaimed.

When their hotel door slammed seconds later, Elena regarded her sister. "You love him, don't you?"

Milán blushed slightly before a toothy grin lit up her face. "I think so."

"By the two-hundred-watt smile just now, I'd say you definitely know." She came over and hugged her sister. "I'm happy for you, Lani. I can't wait to meet him."

"Maybe we'll come for a visit. Adrian has lots of friends in D.C. and it's been a long time since I've been to visit you."

"I'd love that." Elena donned her sunglasses and her purse. "Now, let's go keep an eye on Nyah. She's gone stone crazy since we got here. I think the climate combined with the overabundance of shirtless men has definitely gone to her head.

You'd think this was Vegas," she said and laughed, pushing Milán out the door in front of her.

An hour later, Milán was on a chaise longue sunbathing when her sisters descended on her.

"Milán, *tienes que venir a ver este tipo. El es totalmente guapo.*"

"I'm not going anywhere," Milán replied not bothering to open her eyes. "Besides, I've seen plenty of cute guys today."

Nyah grabbed Milán's bag and started dropping stuff into it. "Not like this. Come on, who knows how long he's going to be there."

"He's definitely worth a peak," Elena agreed.

"I'm not on the market for a boyfriend—I have one."

"Who's not here," Nyah pressed. "So what's the harm in looking? He is an Adonis, Lani."

Milán readjusted her bathing suit as she sat up. "An Adonis?" she snickered. "Fine, I'll go. It seems that's the only way I'll be able to come back and relax."

Nyah smiled in triumph as she handed Milán her bag and hurried off. Milán and Elena had to quicken their pace to catch up with their sister. Nyah slowed as they entered the Port Lucaya Marketplace. With over twelve buildings spread out over several acres, the marketplace was home to many boutiques, restaurants and stores. It overlooked the many boats and yachts docked at the Port Lucaya Marina.

"Okay, we're here." Milán glanced around. "Where is this Greek God?"

"He was heading into one of the restaurants for lunch with some other guy. They're bound to come this way eventually."

Milán sat down at a table. "Nyah, that's a big if."

"*Paciencia,*" her sister implored.

Elena stood up. "You two continue the stakeout. I'm going to get us some drinks."

Their patience was rewarded a few minutes later when a man strolled into the square.

"That's him—Adonis," Nyah whispered loudly. "*Muy delicioso, eh?*"

Milán scrutinized the man walking along at a leisurely pace. She had to admit that Nyah calling him Adonis was definitely warranted. He was Latin, with smoldering looks and a body that would make a woman do almost anything to run her hands over it. His dark, tousled hair only accentuated his appeal. "*Tenías razón. El es precioso,*" she replied.

"*Te lo dije.*"

"Yes, I know you told me," Milán replied shaking her head.

Elena came back and handed each of her sisters a Bahama Mama. "*¡Salud!*"

While Milán sipped her drink, Nyah and Elena argued over the best way to get his attention.

"I'll stroll over and ask him to join us."

"Direct, but what if he says no?" Elena inquired. "You need a backup plan."

Nyah shrugged. "Maybe not. It appears he's got a friend. *Dios mi,*" she groaned. "Look at him."

"Two Adonises in one day?" Elena said with amusement. "I'd say the odds are definitely in our favor."

Milán chuckled and looked up to see the new man her sisters were swooning over. She spit out her drink and dissolved into a fit of violent coughing.

"Oh my goodness." Nyah bolted out of her seat with such force it turned over. She began pounding Milán on the back. "Lani, are you okay?"

"*Respirar,* Milán, *respirar,*" Elena commanded.

Tears ran down Milán's face from all the coughing. She dabbed at her eyes with the damp napkin her drink was sitting on. "That's…no…Adonis," Milán choked out. "That's Adrian."

Through all the commotion, they drew the attention of several passersby, including Adrian and his friend. He did a double take. Striding over to their table, he crouched down in front of Milán with an elated, but worried expression.

"My God, are you okay? What are you doing here? How long

have you and your sisters been in the Bahamas? He was pulling Milán to her feet and into his arms before she'd even answered.

"Adrian," she said, then kissed him. "You said you'd be in the Bahamas, but I didn't know you'd be here," Milán stammered with excitement. "I can't believe it."

Nyah was the first to find her voice. "You're Adrian?"

"Yes, he is." His friend responded for him.

With Milán and Adrian caught up in their own reunion, the other three made introductions.

Finally, Milán turned to the group. "Adrian, I'd like you to meet my two sisters, Nyah and Elena."

"A pleasure to finally meet you." Adrian extended his hand to Nyah, but she batted it out of the way and gave him a big hug.

"We're a family of huggers," she said by way of an explanation.

"So I've heard," Adrian replied before turning to embrace Elena. The guys took two chairs from a nearby table and sat down. Adrian introduced everyone to his friend.

"I'd like you all to meet my friend, and business associate, Tómas Moreno."

"Oh, we've met," Nyah said looking the man over with admiration. "So tell us how you ended up here. I thought you were going to Nassau?" Milán asked.

"We did…are," he told her. "We're just here to look at a few properties." Adrian twisted his fingers around one of her curls. "I never, ever expected to see you here, Lani."

"I didn't know I was going to be here until I reached Miami," she explained. "This is an amazing coincidence."

"So it is," Tómas chimed in. "To find three additional flowers of beauty to add to this tropical paradise is more than any man could hope for."

Elena pursed her lips to hide a smile, but Nyah leaned forward propping her chin in her hands. "Well, aren't you lucky."

"*Muy afortunada*." He grinned.

While the three of them conversed, Milán and Adrian were deep in a conversation of their own. Finally, he stood up and then helped Milán to her feet.

"You all don't mind if we take a walk, do you?"

Elena smiled knowingly. "Not at all. *Hasta luego.*"

Adrian waved and placed his hand at the small of Milán's back. They began to walk.

"So where are you staying?" he inquired when they had more privacy.

"At the hotel across the street. Aren't you staying in Nassau?"

"I was," he corrected.

A smiled brightened her expression. "Was?"

Suddenly, Adrian stopped and placed her in front of him. He watched her closely. "Sweetheart, I realize you're here with your sisters, and I don't mean to interrupt your family vacation but…"

His question was loud and clear. He was asking her to spend the night with him. Milán thought she would have a week to build up to their sleeping together, but things didn't always work out according to plan. The moment their eyes had locked across the courtyard, she knew the week's wait was over. He looked so incredibly sexy, and she had missed him terribly. Fate had intervened to bring them both to this place at this time. There was no way she was going to squander the opportunity for them to be together. She wasn't that crazy.

"Hey?" Adrian squeezed her arm. "Are you in there?"

"Yes, of course," she recovered herself. "Yes."

"Is that yes, you're here, or yes you want to be with me?"

For a split second, Milán thought there was uncertainty in Adrian's expression. *How could he doubt my feelings for him?* she wondered. Not once had she ever seen him display anything but pure confidence and control. Except on a few occasions when he and his mother had not seen eye-to-eye, she corrected herself.

Milán whispered in his ear, "Both," before she nibbled on it.

She felt his hand tighten against her back. "That's going to get you in all sorts of trouble," he said thickly.

"I certainly hope so," she replied saucily.

By the time they returned to the group, Nyah and Tómas were acting like old friends.

"So, what should we do this evening?" Nyah asked the crowd. "Dinner and dancing?"

Adrian sat down and pulled Milán onto his lap. "I'm not sure, but whatever it is, Milán and I will take a rain check."

Chapter 26

With a blush, Milán leaned backward and whispered into Adrian's ear, "Do you have to be so obvious?"

"Damn right, I do," he said aloud. "Sorry all, but we're disappearing."

"Oh, really? Where to?" Milán said excitedly.

"Yes, where indeed?" Elena chimed in.

"I think I might be able to help with that," his friend said standing. "Excuse me a moment while I make a phone call."

Tómas came back less than ten minutes later. "It's all arranged," he said smugly.

"What is?" Adrian asked.

"Your trip. You'll be staying at my rental cottage in Eleuthera."

"What?" Milán's eyes widened. "We couldn't possibly—"

"Yes, you can. It's just a forty-five-minute plane ride to Nassau and then a connecting flight that'll take you right in to Governors Harbour Airport. From there it's a twenty-minute drive to the house. My assistant is booking the flights and rental car as we speak, and the caretaker will meet you at the house to give you the keys."

Adrian set Milán on her feet and stood up. "We can't let you do this," Adrian began.

"Nonsense. It's my pleasure. You flew all the way here to look at properties with me. It's the least I can do."

Nyah took Milán by the elbow and pulled her to the side along with Elena. "Lani, what's the problem? It sounds like a wonderful trip. You should go."

"But what about you two?" Milán frowned. "I can't just up and—"

"Are you crazy?" Elena demanded. "We've been here a few days, and we're having a great time. Don't take this the wrong way, but I think Nyah and I will have plenty of things to keep us occupied while you…hang out with your boyfriend."

Nyah nodded. She looked past her sisters to Adrian's friend. "Milán, you and Adrian need some alone time. Besides, I can just imagine how beautiful Eleuthera is. You need to go get your groove back, Stella. It's time you dusted those pipes off, my dear. The man is hot and you know you want him. As Adrian neared, Nyah switched to Spanish and said, "If anyone needs to get sexed, it's you."

"*¡No puedo creer que hayas dicho que!*" Milán hissed.

"*Creo que debo decirles que puedo hablar en español,*" Adrian said from behind them.

Elena burst out laughing. "*¿Usted habla español?*"

"*Con fluidez,*" Adrian admitted his gaze immediately traveling to Milán.

"What?" Nyah blurted out and then glanced at her sister. "Why didn't you tell us?

"Sorry, I forgot," Milán said quickly.

"You forgot?" Elena chuckled. "I guess you were too busy doing…other things."

"The day we met, your sister cursed me out in Spanish and then tried her best to slam my door off its hinges." Adrian smiled at the memory. "I was pretty angry at that moment, so I didn't let on that I knew what she'd said. Suffice it to say, your sister can use some very colorful metaphors."

"Now that it's all settled, you two have to get moving if you're going to make your flight. Milán, you get packed and I'll bring the car around." Before anyone could protest, Tomás hurried off.

"Wait up," Nyah called out. She turned and gave Elena a pointed look.

"Yeah, we're coming."

Milán watched her two sisters practically run after him. She regarded Adrian. "It seems everything is all arranged."

He gathered her in his arms and kissed her deeply. "Good." His voice caressed her right ear. "Now let's go get into trouble."

Milán packed in record time, said goodbye to her sisters and left with Adrian for the airport. Adrian's friend had thought out every detail. Upon their arrival in Nassau, there was a driver waiting at the airport to escort them to Adrian's resort. He packed his bag and they were off again to catch a flight to Eleuthera. Less than an hour later, they arrived at the Governors Harbour Airport. As promised, the caretaker was there to drive them to their cottage. Their escort passed the time with information about the island and places to eat and visit. Milán only heard half of what the man was saying. Every now and then her thoughts turned to her spontaneous decision to accompany Adrian to an island getaway. Her stomach did a somersault just thinking about the upcoming evening.

"Hey, are you okay?"

She started when Adrian's hand touched hers. "Hmm?"

"I asked if you were okay," he repeated.

"Me? Yes, of course. Why do you ask?"

"Because you looked like you were worried about something."

Milán relaxed her features. "Of course not. I'm just tired, I guess. It's been a long day."

"That's true. Quite a few surprises, too." He smiled.

"I'll say. All good ones." She smiled back.

"We've got some time before we get there. Why don't you try and take a nap?"

Milán decided that sounded like a good idea. Adrian put an arm around her and pulled her into his side. A few minutes later, she was sound asleep.

"Sleeping Beauty, we've arrived." He rubbed her shoulder a few times.

Milán yawned and slowly opened her eyes. She blinked a

few times before glancing out the window. Her jaw dropped. "Adrian, *que es el paraíso!*"

"That it is," he agreed. "Welcome to Eleuthera. Come on, beauty. Let's look around."

The elderly caretaker had stocked the kitchen with food, and mentioned that he was a phone call away if they needed to go into town. Taking their bags into the house, he commenced a guided tour. Milán was surprised at how bright and modern it was. Their cottage had stainless steel appliances, granite countertops and panel doors that recessed into the walls, giving the rear of the house an uninterrupted view of the ocean.

The decor was neutral and calming. The wood furniture was black making a very nice contrast to the white walls and ecru-and-black cushions. While they followed their host around, Milán kept resisting the urge to run out the door and down to the water's edge. The scenery was that beautiful.

They were surprised to hear the cottage had only one bedroom.

"It's a very popular honeymoon destination," the man chuckled cutting a look between them. "Most find that one bedroom is plenty."

He opened the louvered French doors and then he stood aside allowing them to enter. The secluded retreat was at the back of the house, and its biggest asset was the massive four-poster king-sized bed engulfed in a canopy of cream-colored mosquito netting. The regal wood frame monopolized most of the room.

Milán tried to look nonchalant, but it was all she could do to keep her face from turning scarlet as they passed it on their way to the bathroom.

Moments later, the tour had concluded and they were alone. Adrian turned toward her. She tried her best to look like this sort of thing happened to her every day. She failed miserably.

"*¿Tienes hambre?*"

Milán shrugged. "*Un poco.* Did you see the size of that tub?" she said excitedly.

"Yeah. It looked more like a hot tub than a bathtub."

"I know. It's almost as big as the bed."

"Almost," he joked. "Come on," he said taking her hand. "Let's eat."

Taking inventory, they chose a container of conch salad on a bed of lettuce, a fruit plate and some crackers. They decided to dine alfresco. Milán located the plates and silverware while Adrian took the food outside onto the deck. He came back for the wine and two glasses.

By the time he returned, Milán had already fixed their plates. He sat across from her and poured the wine. He held his glass up. "To paradise."

"To paradise," she repeated.

They took a sip and then began eating.

"I have to admit, this was the best idea I've ever had," Adrian said between bites.

"Your idea?" she laughed. "If I recall, it was your friend's plan."

"Yes, but he knew how much I wanted to be alone with you, so when you look at it, I was the catalyst to putting all this in motion."

"You're so full of it," she teased. "Do you have to take credit for everything?"

"Almost everything, yes." He grinned.

"Well done then. Honestly, this place is so beautiful it doesn't seem real." She looked around. "I keep thinking this is just a dream and I'll wake up."

"This is real, Lani." He slid a finger down the top of her hand. "Imagine. We're on a deserted island. It's just the two of us—no interruptions."

Her breath caught in her throat at the flash of desire that swept across his face. She lowered her eyes to her plate.

Adrian studied her. "You aren't sorry you came, are you?"

Her eyes locked with his. "The only thing I'm sorry about is that we have on all these clothes."

Seconds later, she stood up and bolted down the steps and onto the sand. Laughing, she ran toward the water pulling off clothes as she went. By the time she was down to her bathing suit, Adrian was right behind her. He scooped her up and continued running. Milán laughed so hard she starting hiccuping. When he reached the water, he ceremoniously dropped her into the rolling waves.

"It's so warm," she said, once she came up for air.

Diving in, Adrian's powerful arms propelled him effortlessly through the water. He swam a good distance from the shore and then turned back. He stood up and wiped the water from his eyes. The rolling waves crashed into him, but he remained steady. He watched Milán swim toward him. When she reached his side, he scooped her up and held her close for a few moments. A grin played at the corners of his mouth.

Her eyes narrowed. "Don't even—"

Milán didn't get any further. Adrian ceremoniously dumped her into the water.

Sputtering, she came up for air. They began pushing water at each other like little kids—taking turns boasting about their skills. The fight went on for a while longer until Milán declared herself the winner and struck off for the shore.

Adrian sprang into action. He caught up to her in no time and grabbed the back of her leg to reel her in. Kicking and screaming, Milán tried her best to break free. It was futile. With a look of triumph, Adrian wrapped his arms around her waist and spun her around. "Hold still, mermaid. I've caught you fair and square and I'm claiming my prize."

Milán slid her arms around his neck. She let her fingers roam through the wet hair at his nape before drifting lower to squeeze the corded muscles on his back. "*¿Es así?*"

"*Absolutamente.*"

Playtime drifted away with the outgoing tide. Sexual tension swirled around them like the current tugging at their legs. Adrian held her firmly in an iron-tight embrace. When his mouth claimed hers for a kiss, it was with a passion that left no doubt of his intent.

Milán moved her hands over his body. Lowering his mouth

to her neck, Adrian kissed the sensitive area on her collarbone before tracing a path to the beginning of her bikini top.

"*Eso es peligroso, Lani,*" he warned with a low growl.

"*No tengo miedo.*"

Adrian raised his head. He roared with laughter. "You're not scared of me, huh?" His expression held an air of challenge. His thumb moved across the wet material covering her right breast. Her nipples sprang to life. "*¿Estás seguro, Milán?*"

She took a deep breath. Her grip tightened on his forearm, but her eyes never left his. She reached up on her tiptoes and sucked his lower lip into her mouth.

Adrian's reaction was immediate. He groaned and grasped the back of her head letting his fingers wind around her hair to hold her in place. When she released his lip, his returned the favor before moving his tongue past her teeth and into her mouth. She tasted like salt water and mangoes. It was an interesting contrast that made him long to taste more of her.

Unable to help himself, Adrian's dipped his head and kissed the mound of her breast that wasn't covered by her top anymore. His tongue slid over the slick surface of her skin while his hand worked its way lower until it disappeared into the front of her bikini bottom.

"Adrian," she gasped throwing her head back as delectable sensations ricocheted throughout her body.

He leaned over and kissed her. "I'm glad this beach is deserted."

"*No me importa. Te quiero—ahora.*"

His fingers stilled. A wide grin came across his face. "I want you too, *cariño*. Come on," he said grasping her hand. "As amazing as this water is, I think a bed would be a lot better."

Chapter 27

Two thoughts came to mind as Milán watched Adrian remove her bathing suit and then his own. The first was that he was the most handsome and sexy man she'd ever met. The second, and more important, was that she was completely and irrevocably in love with him.

Madre de dios, she lamented to herself. There was no point in denying it. Adrian touched her in ways that she never knew possible. He was exasperating, vain, funny and lovable all at the same time—and he was hers.

The last part was what made her skin tingle and her palms turn moist. They were about to make love and she knew deep down things would never be the same again.

"Hey?" Adrian asked walking up to her. "Are you okay?"

Startled, Milán focused her attention back to the moment. "Yes, I'm sorry," she said quickly. *No zoning in and out now*, she cautioned. She wanted to feel and remember every single detail.

"Sweetheart, are you having second thoughts?" he said with concern.

"Are you crazy?" she blurted out.

They both laughed.

"No, I'm not," she clarified. "I was just daydreaming about how sexy you are and how much I've wanted this—you."

He wrapped his arms around her. "My first thought when I saw you was that you were the most beautiful woman I'd ever seen."

Her eyes sparkled. "My first thought was that your mother wasn't exaggerating. You did have that magnetism that draws a woman in, but then you opened your mouth and ruined it."

There was no way she could contain the laughter the bubbled up at the expression on his face. It was too funny.

"I'll have a hard time living that one down," he chuckled. Milán shrieked with surprise when he swept her off her feet. "It seems I'll have to give you something better to erase that awful memory."

He eased her onto the bed. Adrian knelt there for a moment just looking at her. He raised her hand and kissed the inside of her palm. "Thank you," he said solemnly.

Milán sat up slightly. "For what?"

"For being here. For giving me the chance to tell you how important you are to me."

Getting up on her knees, Milán hugged him. She took his hand and laid it over her heart. Her gaze captured his. "*Muestrame.*"

Adrian nodded and lowered them both back against the plush mattress. He did just as she commanded. He showed her how much she meant to him and he loved every amazing minute of it.

If there was one thing Adrian Anderson was, it was thorough. Milán found out just how much by the detailed way he set out to drive her to the brink of insanity. Adrian studied her body as if she were his greatest work, and he a master artisan. Each caress, kiss and stroke he gave was designed to pinpoint the sensitive areas that excited her and to intensify it.

"Tell me what you want, Lani," he whispered in her ear. "Where should I touch you next?"

Milán raised her hand to her mouth and slid her index finger across her lips. As good as this delicious game was, she wanted much more. "Inside," she told him with a wanton smile.

She took pleasure in seeing the strained look on his face at her brazen declaration. It made her heady to know that she could topple his control with one word like he did hers. Keeping the momentum going, Milán pushed him onto his back. She got up on her knees and hovered over him. Her lips inches away from him. She blew her breath across the hairs on his chest. Adrian tensed.

"But first…a little payback."

Milán let her hand roam from the top of his neck to his stomach. Her fingers splayed across the taut skin learning the feel of him. She felt his muscles flex beneath her as she went lower still.

Adrian closed his eyes. "*Toca me.*"

She did as he asked. Her fingers touched him reverently. Up and down in slow, deliberate motions. Milán watched his face for a reaction. She loved the expressions he was making as she increased the pace. It was intoxicating.

Suddenly, Adrian reached up and stilled her hand. Before she could ask, he had her underneath him. He kissed her fiercely. "I'll be right back."

She watched him roll to the other side of the bed and halfway disappear over the side. "What are you doing?"

He sat up with a box of condoms in his hand.

A blush of excitement crept up her cheeks as she watched him slide a condom on. Pulled tighter than a violin string, Milán was more than ready for the next round to begin. That thought was hammered home when seconds later, he was deep inside her. It felt incredible to finally experience what had kept her up nights, and occupied her thoughts at random moments throughout the day. She held onto him and just reveled in the energy coursing through her body as it stretched to accommodate him. When Adrian began to move faster, Milán wrapped her legs around his waist to increase the sensations.

With each thrust, Adrian took her closer to the edge. He kissed her and repeatedly whispered sentiments into her ear. She loved the sound of his voice. The barely controlled timbre of it as he neared his climax was just as much of a turn-on as them making love. Then she felt it. The warmth. It built inside her, slow and steady like an elevator rising to a higher floor. She held on and waited eagerly for it to eventually hit the top. When it did, Milán called out Adrian's name as wave after wave rolled over her. Adrian was right there with her, holding her tightly until the last spasm ebbed.

Adrian rolled onto his back taking Milán with him. Lying halfway on top of him, she was as satiated as she'd ever been, and for the life of her she just couldn't stop smiling. She raised herself up on her forearms to kiss him. "That was pretty damned incredible," she sighed.

With a flick of his wrist, Adrian smoothed her hair out of her face. "Almost as incredible as the smile on your beautiful face right now," he murmured.

She hugged him. "You put it there."

"Hungry?"

"Uh-uh. You?"

"Nope. I'm doing the only thing I want to do right now."

"Good," she yawned. "Because I'm not moving from this spot."

Adrian stroked her back with his free hand. He listened to her breathing even out.

He wasn't kidding; he was perfectly content to lie there with Milán wrapped around him like a blanket. She felt as delectable as she'd tasted. Finally making love to her had been well worth the wait. Many a night he'd lain awake fantasizing about her. His instincts told him if they ever got together, it would be explosive, and he hadn't been disappointed. Milán Dixon was as fiery in bed as she was out of it.

Adrian stifled a yawn. The tug of sleep was getting too great to ignore. Checking to make sure that Milán was sound asleep, he dislodged himself and rolled over to retrieve the covers. Pulling them over the both of them, he gathered her back into his arms and promptly drifted into a satiated sleep.

Night had approached before either of them stirred. Milán was the first to come fully awake. She sat up in the bed and stretched. Adrian had rolled onto his stomach and was still so she didn't disturb him. She crept as silently as she could out of the bed and padded to the bathroom. A few minutes later, she came out with her hair in a ponytail and feeling refreshed. Deciding to check out the fridge, Milán retrieved a sarong from her bag and slipped it on before heading to the kitchen.

She was perusing the contents of the refrigerator when Adrian's arms snaked around her waist.

"*¿Quién es?*" she asked.

"How soon they forget," he chuckled pulling her against him. He buried his face in her neck. She turned and wrapped her arms around him. "I was hungry."

Adrian raised an eyebrow. "For something other than me? Impossible."

"Good to see your vanity is still in place."

He arched an eyebrow. "That's never going anywhere," he teased before swatting her on the behind. "What do we have?"

Milán rattled off the choices that were quick to make. "How about shish kebabs and a salad?"

"Sounds good to me."

They both prepared the meal. It was such a lovely night; they sat on the deck under candlelight and ate. When they were finished, they took a stroll along the beach. Milán put her feet in the water.

"It's still pretty warm," she said moving farther into the surf.

That was all Adrian needed to hear. Seconds later, he had divested her of the sarong and the two were skinny-dipping under the moonlit sky.

"I've never gone skinny-dipping before," she admitted floating farther out into the water.

"Really? I wonder what else you haven't done?" he said with interest.

He wrapped her legs around his waist and moved lazily around in circles. Milán's arms floated out to her sides keeping her afloat.

"This is amazing," she sighed. "Look at all those stars."

Adrian let his hand move across her flat stomach and higher up to cup her breast. Seconds later she was in his arms. "I'd rather look at you."

They kissed for several long moments before his hand moved underneath the water and found her heat.

"What are you doing?" she moaned aloud.

Adrian's wicked smile shone in the moonlight. "Time to finish what I started."

The next day, they opted to spend their last few hours at the house instead of exploring Eleuthera. While they were stretched out together on a chaise longue, Milán decided to call and check in with her sisters.

"We're doing well," Nyah told her. "We had a wonderful night with Tomás. He took us out to dinner and—"

There was a muffled sound and then arguing.

"Hello?" Milán said into the receiver. "Nyah?"

"Hey, it's me," Elena replied. "Enough about us. How was your night? Was it good? How many times did you—"

"It was great, thanks for asking," Milán said quickly.

"Details later?" her sister pressed.

"Yes, that sounds good."

"Fine," her sister huffed. "When are you two coming back?"

"Tonight. Since Monday is our last night, we decided it would be great for all of us to spend some time together. Adrian would love to get to know you both."

"Uh-huh," her sister replied. "You're crazy. I'd be butt naked and—"

This time Nyah interrupted. They talked a few more moments before Milán hung up.

"Now that was interesting," Adrian chuckled after she returned the phone to the table next to them.

"That's an understatement," she laughed.

His hand drifted down her leg. "So, what did they want to know? All the juicy little details about last night?"

"*Por supuesto*," Milán replied before she rolled over and straddled him. "*Pero no voy a decir.*" She leaned down and kissed him. "So, how much time do we have before we need to leave?"

Adrian glanced at his watch. "About an hour."

"Oh," she pouted. "We've still got to pack, too."

"No, we don't." He grinned. "I packed us up while you were napping earlier."

An excited look crossed her face. "*Excelente,*" she said leaning down for a kiss.

Milán spent the next week in a perpetual state of happiness—and exhaustion. After she and Adrian bid her sisters and his friend goodbye and returned to Chicago, it had been nonstop for both of them. Work was busy, but it was nothing compared to their social calendar. From the moment they returned home, Norma Jean had paraded them around at various functions all over town. She was so happy that they were a couple neither of them had the heart to say no to her events.

"You realize we're going to be at this for a while," Milán said when they were in bed one night.

"We most certainly will not," Adrian contradicted. "My dad called me yesterday and begged me to say no the next time my mother wants us to go somewhere."

"Why?" Milán asked.

"Because he's tired of being her escort to all these things. He's complaining that his TiVo unit only has thirty-three percent of recording time left and that he hasn't watched any of his shows since we got back from the Bahamas."

Milán giggled. "Your poor father."

"Ha, poor us. Between work and the Love Broker, I'm exhausted," he groused.

"*Mi pobre bebé.*" She ran a hand over his bare chest. "What can I do to help?"

Adrian caught her wrist in his hand. He kissed it. Seconds later, she was under him.

"I can think of several things off the top of my head," he said kissing her neck.

"Yeah?"

"Oh yeah," he said thickly. His thumb glided across her breast.

Milán squirmed beneath him. "Adrian," she moaned.

"I'm right here, baby." His hand drifted under her nightgown.

His fingers stroked her with infinite care. It wasn't long before her legs were wrapped around his waist urging him on.

"Tell me what you want? *Dígame lo que usted necesita, cariño.*"

"I need you," she choked out. "*Te necesito. En estos momentos.*"

In record time, Adrian had removed his boxer briefs and her lingerie. When they were both naked, he put a condom on and then sat her on top of him.

Milán loved straddling him. He engulfed her in all the right places and it drove her wild with desire as she moved over him. She was soon rewarded with the sound of him calling her name. That set her over the edge. Unable to take the sweet torture any longer, Milán lost herself in the maelstrom that they'd created. She collapsed against his chest in a heap. Their combined uneven breathing was the only noise in the room.

Adrian wrapped his arms around her and stretched out on the bed.

"That was…"

"Yeah, it was," he said with some effort.

"I'm glad you agree," she replied before lapsing into companionable silence.

Each time they made love, it only got better. Milán wasn't sure how to keep her emotions in check. Who was she kidding? She was way past the point of no return. *El cielo me ayude,* she said to herself. Heaven was going to have to help her, because she loved Adrian more now than the first time they had made love, and nothing on earth was going to change that. "I love you," she said with conviction. Silence ensued.

Milán tilted her head up to find Adrian sound asleep. She smiled. She raised her hand and caressed his cheek. "*Buenas noches, mi amor.*"

Chapter 28

Adrian was in the middle of his weekly staff meeting when his telephone rang. Ignoring it, he continued discussing new goals and objectives for Anderson Realty. Seconds later, his receptionist knocked and poked her head into the office.

"I'm sorry to disturb you, Mr. Anderson, but I have an urgent call for you."

Adrian set his laser pointer down. "Thank you," he said walking over to his desk.

"Give me a minute," he told his team and picked up the phone. After a few seconds, he said, "I'm sorry, everyone, I need to take this."

The team filed out of the office and left him to his phone call.

Later that evening, Adrian met Milán, Justin and Sabrina for dinner.

"I've got some great news," he said after he greeted everyone and sat down. "There's a new opportunity to get in with a loft conversion downtown. They're looking at companies now to be their exclusive agent when the lofts are ready to go on the market."

"Sweetheart, that's incredible news," Milán said excitedly and then kissed him.

"I still have to get used to that," Justin said shaking his head.

"Shut up," Adrian joked.

"Congratulations, Adrian," Sabrina chimed in. "I know Anderson will pull it off."

"We'd better. I heard there are two other companies in the running."

Milán squeezed his arm. "Doesn't matter," she said confidently. "I know we'll win."

He laced his fingers through hers. "I'll do whatever it takes to make that happen."

"So how's the potential new business coming, Milán?" Sabrina asked. "You are still thinking of starting your own company, aren't you?"

"I'm almost ready to go. It's scary and exciting at the same time. Of course I'll be working out of my loft for a while until I find a small office space, but I may already have some potential clients."

Justin whistled. "Wow, so soon? I thought you were still in the planning phase."

"No, I tackled all the business paperwork some time ago. Most of it arrived while we were on vacation. My business cards and promotional materials should be arriving any day now. I've also got a few meetings lined up that could prove promising. Tiffany's even promised to help take some brochures around to local Realtors and businesses for me."

Sabrina hugged her. "I'm so proud of you, Milán. I know you'll do incredibly well."

"You know you don't have to do this right now," Adrian chimed in. "You know you can work at Anderson as long as you like."

Milán smiled. "I know, but you understand that I need to break away now that we are a couple," she reminded him. "Besides, I think it's time I tried to make it on my own. With no safety nets."

Adrian placed a finger under her chin. "*Escucha me.* You will always have a safety net. *¿Comprende?*"

"*Yo sé,*" Milán said kissing him on the lips.

Several seconds later, Justin cleared his throat. The two sat back in their seats, but continued to hold hands.

"So how's Norma Jean?" Justin inquired. "Has she settled down yet or is she still trying to parade you two around town every chance she gets?"

"Definitely getting better," Milán laughed.

"Yeah, she's taking a break," Adrian informed them. "Dad put his foot down."

"I wouldn't get too comfortable," Sabrina warned. "You never know what Jeanie's up to."

After dinner, the foursome walked a few blocks of the Magnificent Mile before the Langleys decided to call it a night. Adrian and Milán waved good-night to their friends and continued on.

"You were kind of quiet after dinner," Milán observed. "Is something wrong?"

Adrian pulled her close. "No, sweetheart. I'm just thinking about the presentation." His thoughts turned to Tony Ludlow. He didn't know if he'd thrown his hat in the ring, but he wasn't taking any chances. Just thinking about the man made him frown.

"Okay, now I know there's something wrong," she told him.

He shook his head. "It's nothing you need to worry about. I'm done thinking about work. The rest of the night it's just us."

Milán looked up at him, but remained silent. *Pick your battles, chica. He'll tell you when he's ready. I hope you're right,* she mused. With that, she turned her attention back to their date.

The next week was a blur of activity at Anderson. The excitement simmering around the office was almost tangible. Adrian worked long hours, and Milán had taken on a few new clients so they hadn't seen much of each other. She missed him. What she wouldn't give to be back on Eleuthera at their private island paradise. Sitting at an outdoor café waiting for her potential client, Milán was looking over the menu when her cell phone chirped. She picked it up off the table and scanned the screen. *Adrian.* She grinned at his suggestion they meet for a midday rendezvous at his place in thirty minutes.

"I can't," she said aloud as she tapped her answer on the screen. I've got an interview. A potential client wants to meet about some upcoming work. It could be big. She typed the last letters in all caps.

Tonight, then?

Milán readily accepted. She typed her reply and then dropped her phone back in her purse.

"Excuse me, are you Miss Dixon?"

She glanced up to see a tall, well-dressed man looming over her.

"Yes, I am," she repeated indicating for him to sit down.

Later that evening, Adrian sat in his bedroom with his feet propped up working on his laptop. He had a consultation in the morning with the developer and had some last-minute details to go over. He was confident that Anderson would win the business and nothing could persuade him otherwise. By this time tomorrow night, he would be out celebrating with Milán, his employees, friends and family. He loved when a plan came together.

His cell phone rang. He grabbed it off the table next to him. "Hello, Mom," he said after checking the Caller ID.

"Hi, honey. I swear you get a girlfriend and you fall off the face of the earth."

Adrian chuckled. "Need I remind you that you've wanted me to do just that for over a year?"

"That's true," Norma Jean agreed. "That hardly means I expect you to forget my phone number—or where we live."

He stared out the window. "Not possible. So what's really bothering you?"

"I just miss my son, that's all," she replied.

He was filling her in on the latest developments at the job when his doorbell rang.

"I'm sorry, Mom, but I have to run. Tell Dad hi for me, and I'll call you tomorrow after the meeting."

"Good luck, honey," she said warmly.

"Luck has nothing to do with it," he joked before hanging up.

Adrian set his laptop on the love seat and went downstairs to answer the door.

When he opened it, Milán was standing on the other side beaming brightly. She threw her arms around his neck and kissed him. They embraced for several moments before Adrian broke contact. "You smell good, and look even better."

"Thank you," she said stepping into the living room. She unbuttoned her coat and slid it off.

"Wow." Adrian whistled. "Is that for me?" he said letting his gaze travel across the black lace teddy she wore.

"All for you," Milán said huskily. She stepped around the

coat and straight into his arms. She kissed him thoroughly, her hands sliding up his back to yank his shirt out of his slacks. "We have some celebrating to do," she informed him.

"Really?"

"Mmm-hmm," she replied undoing the buttons on his shirt. "I got my first freelance job. I'll be the design consultant for a real estate company downtown."

"That's my girl." Adrian hugged her. He took her hand and they went upstairs. He set her down in front of the bed. "So, what's the job?"

"It's supposed to be huge. We're talking very high-end condos. My client wants me to stage them." Her arms slid around his neck. "It'll be great exposure for me."

"Is that so? You know there are other parts of you I'd like to see exposed right about now," he said kissing her neck.

Before Milán could respond Adrian's cell phone rang.

"Damn," he muttered. "I'm expecting a call, but I'll be brief."

"You'd better."

With a swish of her hips, Milán sank down on the bed and watched him.

"Hold that thought," he said before hitting the talk button on his phone.

"Hey, man. Now's not the best time—" he began, but stopped after a few seconds. "What? Okay, but make it quick."

After another moment, his face dropped. "Are you sure?"

Milán sat up and stared worriedly at Adrian.

After he hung up, Adrian scooted his laptop out the way and sank down onto the love seat with the cell phone still in his hand. Utterly still, his jaw clenched rhythmically.

"Adrian?" Milán scooted to the edge of the bed. "What is it?"

He looked over at her. Anger hardened the lines of his face. "The company that just hired you—what's the guy's name?"

"Anthony Ludlow. Why?"

Standing, Adrian tossed his phone onto the couch. "Tony Ludlow hired you."

"Yes," she said patiently. "I don't understand why you—"

"That bastard's trying his best to piss me off," he snapped.

Surprise registered on her face. "You know him?"

"Of course I know him," he said impatiently. "He's Anderson's biggest competitor, Milán."

She stood up. "What? Why didn't you tell me?"

"How was I supposed to know you'd accept a position with that jackass?"

"How was I to know the two of you were rivals?"

"I'm sure he must've mentioned it," Adrian countered.

"No…he didn't."

The censure in her voice only made him more annoyed. After all, he had forbidden his employees from mentioning Ludlow's name in his own damn office. He started pacing across the floor, a string of curses littering the air behind him. Milán resumed her seat on the edge of the bed and watched him.

After a full minute of Adrian's tirade, she said, "Why do you let this man get to you so much?"

He stopped and stared at her. "Ludlow makes it a point to go after what I want. He never misses an opportunity to try and get the upper hand."

"What are you saying?"

"Come on, Milán. It's well-known that you work for me, and he could probably find out that we're a couple. It's hardly rocket science," he said drily. "He's not sincere about that job offer. He's just keeping his enemies close to try and find a weakness and then exploit it. He thinks he's found one by hiring my girlfriend."

"Gee, it appears you don't think much of my professional abilities," she snapped.

"Of course I do, but this isn't about your professional abilities, trust me."

"How can you be sure?"

"Because I know Tony Ludlow. He doesn't make a move without ensuring it keeps him one step ahead. But it doesn't matter. He won't gain the edge he's looking for. Tomorrow you're going to tell him where he can stick his job offer."

"What?"

"You'll quit and then let him know his plan to gain an edge

over Anderson fell short." Adrian smiled. "I can see the SOB's face when you—"

"I'm not quitting."

He raised an eyebrow. "Excuse me?"

"I have an agreement with him, Adrian. He's my client. I just can't back out after agreeing to be his designer. I gave him my word."

"Are you crazy? Your word was given under false pretenses. He doesn't want you to design anything. He's hoping to do reconnaissance on what Anderson's strategy is to win listing for the condos."

Anger flared in her eyes. "Do you know how insulting you sound right now? You're saying that he doesn't care about my abilities, and that I got this job not on my own merit, but by the fact that you and I go together."

"Uh, yeah." He crossed his arms. "That about covers it."

"*Que son ridículas*," she said hotly.

"I'm ridiculous?" he thundered. "You don't see how you working for him looks from my side, or to my staff? What part of this doesn't make sense, Milán?"

"You know, I'm not sure which is worse. Your vanity or your paranoia."

His jaw tightened. "This has nothing to do with vanity, and I'm sure as hell not paranoid."

She threw her hands up in disgust. "This is pointless."

"I'm glad you agree. So you'll tell him you've changed your mind."

A determined look crossed her face. "No, I'm not. I've given my word, and I'm not about to take that back because you have a problem with Anthony Ludlow."

His expression was serious. "I'm telling you, Tony can't be trusted and he'll use you to his advantage. You're either on my side on this or you aren't, Milán. As my girlfriend, I would think this wouldn't be that hard a decision."

She stepped back. "You're right, Adrian. It isn't. The bottom line is you don't trust me enough to know that I would never spy on you, or do anything that would hurt you—or your company. So I guess I'm done."

"What the hell does that mean?" he asked softly.

"It means we're through."

"You can't be serious," he said skeptically. "You're willing to break up with me over a difference of opinion? It's our first argument, Milán, and you're throwing in the towel already and I'm the one with loyalty issues?"

"It's more than that and you know it. You don't respect me—or my abilities."

"It's not your abilities I'm questioning," he shot back. "It's his."

"I'm able to keep business separate from pleasure—sadly it seems you can't."

He watched her go. "This is stupid," he said aloud.

She left without saying another word. After a few moments, Adrian heard his front door close forcefully. Milán had really left. *Well one thing's certain, I'm sure as hell not chasing after her,* he told himself. With a loud expletive, Adrian sank onto the couch and put his feet up. After a few moments, he ran a hand over his jaw. Picking up his cell phone, he dialed Justin's number and waited. When his friend picked up, Adrian filled him in on his blowup with Milán.

"You should let things cool off before talking to her again," Justin cautioned. "Give it some time."

"This makes no sense at all. Hopefully she'll realize her mistake by morning, tell Ludlow where to go and then we'll patch things up."

"You're sure about that?"

"Of course," he said tersely. "I know Milán won't risk what we have over this."

"For your sake, I hope you're right," his friend replied.

"Of course I'm right, Justin. If it's one thing I know, it's women."

Chapter 29

Norma Jean eyed her son over her coffee mug. She shook her head. "Do you know anything about women?"

Adrian let out an impatient breath. He'd been hearing this comment or something similar for the last two weeks. It was grating on his nerves.

"Mom, we've been over this hundreds of times. Milán broke up with me, not the other way around. I'm sure she'll come to realize her mistake and she'll fix this."

"Oh, wake up," his mother snapped. "I'd say that ship has sailed. You haven't seen or talked to Milán since she left. Every time I speak with the poor girl, she sounds more and more distant. She's a good friend of mine, and this stupid quarrel of yours is starting to affect our relationship."

"Stupid?" Adrian's temper flared. "She went to work for Ludlow, Mom. What's worse, she refused to quit even after I told her about him."

"If he was such an issue, you should've told her from the start, but we all know how you love to keep stuff to yourself when it has anything to do with work—and to make matters worse you ordered her to give up her first client."

He bristled. "I can't believe you're trying to turn this around on me. And besides, I didn't order her—I asked."

"I heard the recap, Adrian. You demanded."

He threw his hands up. "So what if I did? What if I worked

with someone I used to date? You don't think Milán would have a problem with that?"

"Considering that's probably half the unmarried women in Chicago, why would she? Besides, she'd never met Tony Ludlow, much less gone out with him."

Adrian pushed away from the table. "This conversation is getting us nowhere. My relationship with Milán will either work out, or it won't. I've tried calling her, but she won't pick up. That speaks volumes."

"Maybe she can sense that you aren't sincere about getting her back."

"She's the one that walked out on me. It was our first argument and she hightails it out the door? That tells me we weren't as solid as I thought."

"Nonsense," his mother countered. "You have to work this out without playing the blame game."

"Thanks for the insight," he said standing up. "But I'm not the one that bolted." He laughed without humor. "Kind of ironic isn't it, considering my track record?"

"If you ask me—"

"I didn't."

"You're both at fault," she finished. "So you both need to fix it."

Adrian walked around the table and kissed his mom on the cheek. "I love you, Mother, but I'm begging you to stay out of it. I'm going to say goodbye to Dad. I'll see you for dinner on Thursday, okay?"

She huffed, but nodded. Norma Jean watched her son walk out of the kitchen. Setting her cup down on the table, she tapped it absentmindedly.

"I know that look, Jeanie," her husband said from the door. He came in and sat across from his wife. "Don't stir up any trouble," Heathcliffe cautioned. "You promised Adrian you wouldn't interfere."

"I did no such thing. He said he was coming over for dinner, and I nodded."

"Jeanie—"

"Don't start, Cliff. Our son's in love with Milán Dixon. I can see it in his eyes. He may be too pigheaded to realize it on his own, but a mother knows."

"That may be true," Heathcliffe countered, "but it's his life. He's got to live with the decisions he makes."

"Yeah, well, it's affecting us, too, and if you think I'm going to just sit around and watch Adrian screw up his chance at happiness and giving me grandbabies, you can think again."

The telephone chirped loudly causing Milán to grab the stepladder she was on for support. "Good grief," she gasped with shock.

Taking one step at a time, she got down and turned off the vacuum cleaner and set the telescopic cleaning attachment onto the floor. She walked over to the coffee table and picked up her cell phone.

"*Hola,* Nyah. *¿Qué tal?*"

"*Muy bien.* The question is, how are you?"

"Good," Milán said in a chipper voice.

"Are you sure?" her sister persisted.

"Yes, I am, so quit asking. I broke up with Adrian. I didn't have major surgery."

"You're right, what was I thinking? You were only crazy about the guy. Why in the world would I think you weren't over it? So tell me, sis, what are you doing?"

Closing her eyes, Milán pursed her lips. "Just some tidying up."

"Tidying, huh. *¿Qué?*"

"Not much, just vacuuming my walls."

Silence ensued.

"You know, to get cobwebs out of the ceilings."

"*Madre de Dios,*" her sister replied and then burst into laughter. "You've got it bad."

Justin called Adrian a few days later and invited him to dinner.

"I won't be good company," he replied in a surly tone.

"We'll chance it," his friend replied. "We haven't seen you in a while."

"Work's got me busy," Adrian hedged.

"All the more reason to get out. Come on, man."

"Fine. What time?"

An hour later, Justin, Sabrina and Adrian were at Francesca's.

"Isn't this great?" Sabrina remarked. "The food's delicious and there's a nice crowd tonight."

Justin leaned in. "Quite a bit of eye candy, too."

Adrian perused the room. "Hadn't noticed." He dug into his pocket and retrieved his ringing cell phone. "It's work," he said getting up from the table. "Be right back."

As he stepped outside to take the call, Adrian collided with the person coming in.

"Sorry," he said automatically.

The smile faded when he saw Milán standing in front of him. *Damn.* He muttered to himself. "Sorry but I need to call you right back," he said before hanging up.

They stood staring at each other. Milán was the first to recover.

"Hi."

"Hey," he replied.

Strained silence enveloped them like a canopy. Someone was trying to squeeze by so they came inside.

"How've you been?"

"Good," she said. "You?"

"Just fine. How's the new job?"

"Doing well. Tony and his staff have been great."

Any semblance of cordiality dissolved at the mention of Ludlow's name.

"You must be thrilled," he said bitingly. "Excuse me, I've got a call to return."

Adrian strode out the door before she could reply.

Spotting Justin and Sabrina when she came in, Milán walked over to say hello.

"You just missed Adrian." Sabrina told her.

"We ran into each other. Literally." She glanced over her shoulder. Adrian was heading back into the restaurant. "Well, I have to run. I'm meeting a friend for dinner. It was great seeing you both," she said cheerfully.

"You, too," Sabrina replied.

Unfortunately for Milán, when she sat down at her table, she noticed it afforded her a clear vantage point of Adrian's table. *It's only his profile. At least he's not right across from you,* her conscience pointed out.

"I had no idea we'd run into Adrian," Tiffany said nervously. "Are you okay?"

"It's no big deal. It was bound to happen sooner or later," Milán said dismissively. Picking up her menu, she glossed over the selections. Seconds later, she peeped over the top of it to view Adrian. He was laughing at something Justin had said. Her stomach flittered. She lowered her gaze.

Tiffany followed her line of sight. "Milán, do you want to move to another table?"

She jumped. "Hmm? Uh, no, of course not."

"Are you sure? Seeing him can't be easy."

Milán looked toward his table again. "Hey, I'm a big girl, I can handle it. He and I are ancient history, right? No big deal."

By the time their meal came to an end, Milan had managed to walk past them to the ladies' room without incident. She was a bundle of nerves, but it didn't show on the outside. When she got back to her table, Tiffany had paid the bill and had their leftovers in doggie bags.

"You didn't have to do that," Milán protested. "At least let me leave the tip."

"Fair enough. I figured I'd save us some time," she replied standing up.

Milán found out their haste was unnecessary. By the time they headed to the entrance, Adrian and his friends were gone. As they walked back to Tiffany's car, Milán kept up constant chatter. She discussed her latest client, the movie she'd treated herself to the other night and the trouble she'd had trying to convince her family that her life wasn't coming to an end because of her breakup with Adrian. "I mean, really, I don't know why they keep harping on it. I can tell by the tone in their voices when they call. Everyone is expecting me to break down and wallow in self-pity. Well, I'm not doing it. I'm perfectly fine."

"Yeah, I can see that," Tiffany replied getting into the car.

Milán slid into the passenger seat and buckled her seat belt. "What's that supposed to mean?"

"Look, I may not have known you that long, but it's enough to know that this," Tiffany said waving her hand toward Milan, "overly perky attitude of yours isn't fooling a soul."

"I don't know how many times or different ways I can say I'm over him, Tiff."

Her friend looked at her. "It's not me you have to convince, Milán," she observed. "It's yourself."

Milán was viewing her design plan for her client when Tiffany's words replayed in her head. *It's yourself you have to convince.* Frustrated, she threw her pencil down and leaned back in her chair. The last three weeks had been a blur since she'd been hired by Anthony Ludlow. Her new client was cordial, knowledgeable and smart, but something was missing. Truthfully, he just didn't have the same electricity she'd felt while working with Adrian at Anderson Realty. *Admit it, you miss him,* she told herself. Seeing him at Francesca's was like ripping a Band-Aid off a wound.

It was true. She did miss Adrian. Everything about him in fact: the way he bragged about how perfect he was, or how dedicated he was to his company and employees. The way he looked at her with such passion it made her breathless. Just picturing the two of them making love made desire flare up inside her like a wildfire.

"This is getting me nowhere," Milán complained aloud. *Except wanting him.* Her thoughts betrayed her. So did her heart. She was miserable without him near, but there was no way she'd just roll over and forgive him. He'd been dead wrong about Ludlow. Not once had he asked about Adrian's organization and how it functioned. Tony Ludlow was only interested in his own business and how Milán's expertise enhanced it.

Just thinking about it made her mad all over again. Bolting out of her chair, Milán grabbed her purse and keys. Suddenly, her cell phone rang. She glanced at the screen and grimaced.

"Hi, Jeanie," she said, trying to sound chipper.

"Hey, honey, how are you?"

"Just fine and you?"

"Good considering I haven't seen you in several weeks."

Milán was contrite. "I'm sorry. I haven't been much of a friend lately. Please forgive me."

"Of course. Especially if you come over this evening, and before you say no," she said quickly, "the boys have gone out so we'd be alone."

"I don't know, Jeanie."

"It'll be great to have a girls' night. You wouldn't deny an old woman, would you?"

"Okay," Milán laughed. "I'll be there shortly."

"Great," Norma Jean said excitedly. "I've cooked up a fantastic meal and I've made your favorite—banana pudding."

She shook her head. "So you knew I'd say yes, huh?"

"Nonsense. I only hoped you would. See you shortly."

Milán had to chuckle. Norma Jean was used to getting her way. Just like another person she knew.

Sitting in Andy's Jazz Club, Adrian glanced between his father and his best friend. "Is this supposed to be your attempt at an intervention?"

"More like an observation," Justin replied. "Admit it, you're miserable without her."

"I'm not miserable," Adrian retorted.

"You've been cranky, preoccupied and short-tempered, but definitely not miserable," his father chuckled sipping his drink.

"Look, I know you both mean well, but can we change the subject?"

"Well, I heard the Love Broker has dusted off her black book," Justin said casually.

"What?" Adrian and his father said simultaneously.

Justin nodded. "Sabrina told me Jeanie's fixing Milán up with one of the nephews of her choir member. What was his name?... Michael... Martin..."

Adrian sat up ramrod straight. "What the hell are you talking about?"

"Jeanie said it's time Milán got back on the market. She said since your relationship has ended, there's no sense in both of you sitting home pining."

Adrian's face turned red. "I'm not pining. I've had plenty of stuff going on."

"Yeah, work...yelling at people...work," Justin snickered.

"Shut up," Adrian snapped.

After a few moments of deafening silence, Justin whistled and started laughing at Adrian.

"What's funny?"

"I think you're going to give me twenty dollars."

"Excuse me?"

"We made a bet a long time ago, remember? I bet you that love was going to bite you one day. You said it wouldn't."

With a grunt, Adrian downed his beer. "So?"

"So, son, I think you owe Justin some money." Heathcliffe grinned.

Adrian impatiently signaled the waitress for their check. "What I think is that my mother and I are going to clear the air—right now."

Chapter 30

Norma Jean came into the dining room with a flourish. "I hope you're ready for dessert."

"I'm stuffed," Milán protested.

Norma Jean set a glass bowl in front of her. "There's always room for dessert."

She sat down and the two began chatting again.

"Milán, I wish you'd reconsider letting me fix you up. He's a wonderful man that really knows how to treat a lady," Norma Jean told her.

"Jeanie, the last thing I need right now is to go out on a date."

"What date?"

Milán choked on her pudding at the loud voice. She sputtered and wiped her mouth with her napkin. She glanced up to see Adrian hovering in the doorway glaring at them.

Norma Jean said, "Adrian, what a nice surprise."

"You're fixing Milán up with some guy from church?" he said without preamble.

"Would you like some dessert, sweetheart?"

"No, I don't want dessert," he said tersely. He strode over to the table. "Mother, you promised me you'd butt out."

"I did no such thing, and I think you'd better change your tone. I'm still your mother," she admonished.

"Apparently you're also a dating service."

Milán got up from her chair. "*Adrian, ¿podemos hablar de esto más tarde?*"

"No, we're not going to talk about this later," he replied. Before she could say more, the doorbell rang.

"I'll get it," Norma Jean said quickly. "I'm expecting—"

"I know who you're expecting," Adrian thundered. "I'll get it."

He brushed past his father and went to answer the door. He wrenched the door open and stood there. "What?"

"Hi… Uh, is Mrs. Anderson here? I'm—"

Adrian eyed the man with disdain. "Let me guess, Michael? Or was it Martin?"

"No, I'm Larry."

"Listen, Larry, there's been a mistake. I don't care what my mother told you, Milán isn't going out with you—period."

The man stood there with his mouth open. "I'm not—"

"Adrian," Norma Jean called from the hallway. She pushed past him. "Knock it off. Larry's here to drop off the church bulletins," his mother informed him.

His gaze traveled between his mother and the man standing on the porch. "Really. At this hour?"

Larry held out a box toward Norma Jean. "Here you go, Mrs. Anderson."

"Thanks, dear. Thank Sister Mabel for me and tell her I hope she's feeling better."

"I will, ma'am," Larry said before hurrying down the steps.

Norma Jean shut the door and turned on her son. "Have you lost your mind?"

Adrian did a double take. "Me? What about you?"

"How about we all sit down and discuss this." Heathcliffe came up behind them.

"The only thing I'm interested in discussing is how my mother thought it was a brilliant idea to fix up my girlfriend with another man."

Norma Jean snorted. "What girlfriend? You tossed her aside. Or have you forgotten?" She huffed, and then strode back into the dining room.

Adrian was right on her heels. "I didn't…that is not what happened, and you know it. Milán was the one that ended things."

"Because you were trying to roll over her like a steam engine," his mother shot back. "As usual."

"Where did you get that idea? I never once treated Milán that way."

"You sure about that?" his mother quipped.

"Will you both stop talking about me like I'm not here?" Milán said loudly.

Everyone turned to stare at her.

"I'm sorry, dear," Norma Jean apologized.

"That happens a lot in this house," Adrian said cynically.

"Pardon my son's uncouth behavior."

Adrian rolled his eyes. "Completely unwarranted, right, Mother?"

"Well it was you that jumped to conclusions about who was at the door. If you'd have let me get a word in, you would've known it wasn't Milán's date."

The doorbell chimed again.

Adrian sighed. "Who's that, the pastor?"

A smug look crossed his mother's face. "No, *that* is Milán's date."

"What?" Milán gaped in surprise. "Jeanie, you didn't. I didn't agree to this."

Adrian shook his head. "Why would my mother ever let something trivial like a person's wishes get in the way?" He glanced at his mother. "You should answer the door. If I do, I guarantee things won't turn out the way you planned."

He turned to Milán. "*Tenemos que hablar. Ahora, por favor.*"

"*No tengo nada que decir,*" she said wearily.

"*Es muy importante.*"

"Fine." She glanced over at his parents. "Please excuse us. Apparently, your son has something important he needs to say."

Milán followed Adrian out onto the deck. The night air was a bit chilly, but she refused to say she was cold. Suddenly, she felt a coat around her. She glanced over her shoulder. "Thank you."

"You're welcome." Adrian walked in front of her.

Milán couldn't help the surge of excitement at seeing him.

It was the same euphoric feelings she got biting into a fresh-out-of-the-oven empanada or anything with warm gooey chocolate. *Stay focused. Say what you need to say and leave,* her brain warned.

"I didn't know you'd be here."

"Your mother invited me for dinner—it was last-minute." His mouth raised into a wry smile. "With my mother I doubt that very seriously. Especially since Prince Charming is pounding on the door."

She bristled at his tone. Milán walked past him and sat down. She inhaled a deep breath and regretted it. Her nostrils were flooded with Adrian's scent mixed with cologne that lingered on his jacket. *Great,* she muttered to herself. Undercurrents of desire began to flow through her. She shifted several times in her chair before she said, "So what is it you have to say, Adrian?"

"Did you know about this date?" he demanded.

"Of course not," she said hotly. "Jeanie invited me to dinner. How would I know a man was going to show up at the door—twice."

"So you didn't ask her to do this?"

"No," she said indignantly. "Why would I?"

"To make me jealous," he countered.

Milán bolted to her feet. "Does everything have to be about *you*? No, I'm not trying to make you jealous, Adrian. You've made it abundantly clear how you feel about me, and who I'm working for."

"Actually, that's not entirely true. I've told you how I feel about you working for Ludlow—not how I feel about you."

She felt like she'd been suckered punched, but Milán held her ground.

"Oh, you've told me, Adrian. You don't trust me. You don't think I can get a job on my own merit. By the way, you were wrong about Anthony Ludlow. Not once did he ask me anything about you, your company or what you had planned. So you can stop worrying that I'm going to spy on you the first chance I get."

"You're putting words in my mouth."

"If I am, they're to match your accusations from a few weeks ago," she threw back at him.

"I apologize for that," he said with remorse. "Things didn't come out right."

"So you're not sorry for what you said, only how you said it." She shook her head. Taking off his jacket, Milán handed it to him and moved to leave.

He reached out to stop her. "Wait a minute. We need to talk about this."

"We've talked, Adrian, and you were dead wrong."

"Fine, I was wrong about him—that time."

"I can't believe you," she yelled. "You know what? Forget it. It's a moot point anyway."

Adrian's expression darkened. "What's that supposed to mean?"

"I'm moving back to Miami."

"The hell you are," he thundered. Adrian ran a hand over his jaw. Anger flooded his system. He turned away from Milán to get his emotions in check. It took considerable effort, but he tried again. "Why are you leaving?"

She shrugged. "I love it here, but... *Echo de menos a mi familia.* I thought I could get acclimated to not seeing them so often, but it hasn't worked out that way."

Adrian cocked his head to the side. "And that's the only reason?"

"*Absolutamente.*"

His smile was telling. "*Estás mintiendo.*"

She placed her hands on her hips. "Why would I lie?"

"Because we've got unfinished business, *cariño.*"

She stepped back. "I can't imagine what that would be."

Adrian moved across the deck. She retreated until her backside brushed against the deck railing. He reached up and cupped her chin. "I said I was sorry, Lani."

"You didn't mean it, Adrian."

"I did—and do. I realized I was wrong to give you an ultimatum, Milán. You taking Ludlow as a client came as a shock.

I reacted badly. Whom you choose to work for is completely your decision. I overstepped my boundaries by trying to dictate what you should do. It's your business, and your decision."

Milán's jaw dropped. "What have you done with Adrian Anderson," she blurted out.

His laughter echoed around them. "I thought it wise to step out of character for once."

"I should have, too," she confessed. "I'm way too hotheaded."

"You had a right to be angry with me." He slid a hand up her shoulder. "You're damn good at what you do, Milán. I was out of line to suggest Ludlow wanted you for anything but that. He's a fool if he doesn't appreciate the gem he has."

"He does," she told him.

Adrian tensed and released her. "Good. I'm glad things are going so well for you, and that my suspicions were off base."

Milán smiled. "I didn't exactly say that."

"Is something wrong? Did Ludlow—"

"No, it's nothing like that," she replied trying to calm him. "I just…well… It's not the same," she admitted. "Working with him is fine, but it's definitely not like at Anderson."

He pulled her closer. "So you missed me."

"I missed everyone," she corrected.

Adrian's smile eclipsed the moon. "But mostly me."

"Especially you."

Tracing the outline of her lips with his finger, he said, "I seem to have that effect on people."

Her eyes rolled heavenward. "Yeah, I'll bet."

Milán wasn't sure who made the first move, but they ended up solidly in each other's arms. She held onto him and relished the feel of being wrapped in his warm embrace.

"I'm sorry about the way I ended things. I just got overwhelmed by everything. I was so worried history was repeating itself and I was making a huge mistake. I was… I was scared my heart would get broken again and I panicked."

Adrian tilted her face up so they were eye-to-eye. "Milán, I would never intentionally hurt you. Earlier, my mother accused me of steamrolling over you. That truly wasn't my intent. Forgive me if I made you feel that way."

She hugged him tightly. "I've missed you," she said softly.

"I've missed you, too," was his muffled reply before his mouth descended on hers.

He kissed her cheek and traveled down her neck with his lips. Eventually, Adrian lifted her off the ground and wrapped her tightly in his arms.

"You left at the first sign of trouble, Milán. If you ever break up with me like that again —"

"I won't," she vowed. "Ever."

"Good, because I love you, Milán, and I want you to stay with me."

Milán gasped. "*¿Tú me amas?*"

Adrian kissed her. "Of course I love you. How could you doubt it? You think I'd apologize to just anybody?"

She poked him in the stomach. "Adrian Anderson, you are the most obnoxious, vane, know-it-all man I've ever met in my life."

He grinned as if she'd just complimented him. "And?" he prodded.

She tilted her head back and shouted, "And I'm completely in love with you."

"So you're staying?"

"Yes," she said loudly. "I'm staying here in Chicago."

Adrian hugged her tightly. "*Fantástico.*"

"And I'm giving Anthony Ludlow my two weeks' notice."

"Even better," Adrian said approvingly. "So, when are you coming back?"

"I'm not," Milán informed him. "I'm still working for myself."

"That's too bad," he said in a serious tone. "I was looking forward to sleeping with my subordinate again."

She poked him in the ribs. "*Eres ridículo.*"

"I know." Adrian kissed her until they were both breathless. "It's a good thing you're staying because I'd hate to have to fly all the way to Miami just to ask you to marry me."

Milán was as still as a statue. "*¿Qué dice?*"

"I said I'd hate to have to—"

"The other part," she interrupted.

"The one where I asked you to marry me?"

"Yeah, that part," she said in a shocked whisper.

Adrian got down on bended knee. Milan covered her mouth with both hands.

"Milán, I love you. You mean everything to me. You're my soul mate, my lover and the first, and only, best female friend I've ever had. I want to spend the rest of my days making you happy and sharing my life with you. Please do me the honor of becoming my wife."

Before she could respond, he repeated the entire proposal in Spanish. She burst into tears.

"When did you have time to buy a ring?" she sniffed as he slid a diamond engagement ring onto her left ring finger.

"Sweetheart, I've had three weeks to realize what an ass I've been. That gave me plenty of time to window shop. You weren't getting away twice."

"But…but you didn't know I'd be here."

"Justin let it slip that the Love Broker was at it again. So I decided it was time for my mother to retire that damned black book once and for all. From there we made a pit stop at my place so I could get your ring."

Milán glanced up. "So everyone knows?"

Adrian kissed her ring finger. "No, Lani. I wanted this moment to be just between us—like our island paradise. Which reminds me," he said staring at her.

She wiped some of the tears from her eyes. "Yes?"

"You haven't answered my question. Are you going to marry me, or what?"

"Oh. Yes, yes, yes," she cried. "I can't wait to be your wife, Adrian. I love you so much."

He tenderly brushed the tears away with his thumb. "Good answer."

They sealed their vow with a kiss. Adrian picked up his coat and placed it back on her shoulders.

"Let's go break the news."

"Your mother is going to pass out," Milán said against his lips.

"It's possible," he chuckled. "I think we'd better tell her in the Cupid room."

"Why?" Milán inquired. "Because the family room is the most romantic?"

"No, because it has the thickest carpet."

Chapter 31

Norma Jean wrapped her arms around her husband's neck. "It's been ages since we've danced together. Who'd have thought we still had it?"

"Yeah, it's been two whole weeks," Heathcliffe said twirling her around and back into his arms. "Glad neither of us has gotten rusty."

Norma Jean laughed. "Oh, darling, I'm having such a good time," she told him.

"Excuse me, do you mind if I cut in?"

Heathcliffe released his wife and stepped aside. "She's all yours, son."

Adrian took his mother in his arms and spun her around the dance floor. "You look happy."

She smiled up at him. "Honey, how could I not be having a wonderful time?"

"I'm glad. I wanted to make sure everyone knows I'm off the market, and that your matchmaking days are finally over. You will be hanging up the Love Broker hat, and throwing away that little black book," he replied sweetly. "Just like you promised."

"Anything for you, darling. I'm so glad things worked out with Milán. I almost had a coronary when I saw that ring on her finger. You made your mother so happy."

"I am too, Mom. Who would've thought that I'd settle down?" he said in awe. "But I guess some things even sneak up on me."

"I couldn't be more pleased. She's going to make a wonderful daughter-in-law," Norma Jean said confidently. "I can't wait to meet her family. I've been practicing my Spanish, too." She winked. "I'm just sorry they couldn't make it for the party."

"They'll be coming in a few days. Milán wanted to make sure Pia was completely over that stomach flu before they traveled." He squeezed his mother's hand. "You know, if someone had told me last year I'd be getting married as soon as humanly possible, I would've thought them insane," he said in awe. "And yet, here we are."

His mother's eyes grew wide. "I didn't think to ask, and not that it matters in the least, but, Adrian, is she—"

"No, Mom," he said quickly. "Milán isn't pregnant. I think we'll get used to being married a while before we talk grandbabies—if that's okay with you?"

"You'd better get to it," she warned him. "I'm not getting any younger."

"Or quieter," he teased.

Justin walked over and handed his wife a glass of champagne. "Having fun?"

"Yes, it's a lovely engagement party," Sabrina replied. "Another success for the Love Broker."

He kissed her hand. "We're living, breathing married proof that Jeanie's matchmaking works."

Sabrina observed Milán and Adrian on the dance floor. "And now we've got another happy couple to add to the list. I guess Jeanie's matchmaking days are over."

Justin's gaze traveled to Adrian's mother. "Uh-huh. I'll believe it when I see it."

"So will I," Tiffany said over the shoulder of her date.

"You'd better watch out, Tiffany," Sabrina warned. "You're still single."

"So?" she replied.

"So," Justin chimed in. "That makes you fair game in Norma Jean's eyes. "You'd better watch your back," he said with a chuckle.

The smile dropped from Tiffany's face. She glanced warily

over to where Adrian's parents were dancing, and then back to Sabrina and Justin. "Seriously?"

Adrian leaned down and kissed his fiancée. "*Te amo.*"

"I love you, too," she grinned. "You realize you're stuck with me and my obsessive cleaning habits forever."

"I don't mind," he said casually. "Personally, I can't wait to discover what other things you do to perfection. If those hidden talents are anything like the ones we discovered in the Bahamas, we'll never see family and friends again."

Milán giggled. "We can't forget what we learned in the Bahamas. Do you really want to be the one to tell Norma Jean she'll have to rent grandbabies after all?"

They both looked over at his mother and burst out laughing. Adrian shuddered. "Baby, I'm in love, not crazy."

* * * * *

Two classic Eaton novels in one special volume...

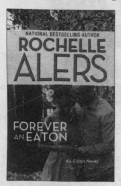

FOREVER
AN EATON

NATIONAL BESTSELLING AUTHOR
ROCHELLE ALERS

In *Bittersweet Love,* a tragedy brings history teacher Belinda Eaton and attorney Griffin Rice closer when they must share custody of their twin goddaughters. Can their partnership turn into a loving relationship that is powerful enough to last?

In *Sweet Deception,* law professor Myles Eaton has struggled for ten years to forget the woman he swore he'd love forever—Zabrina Cooper. And just when Myles is sure he's over her, Zabrina arrives back in town. As secrets are revealed, can they recapture their incredible, soul-deep chemistry?

"Smoking-hot love scenes, a fascinating story and extremely likable characters combine in a thrilling book that's hard to put down." —RT Book Reviews on SWEET DREAMS

Available May 2013 wherever books are sold!

www.Harlequin.com

REQUEST YOUR FREE BOOKS!

2 FREE NOVELS
PLUS 2 FREE GIFTS!

KIMANI™
ROMANCE

Love's ultimate destination!

Fan-favorite author

ZURI DAY

PLATINUM
Promises

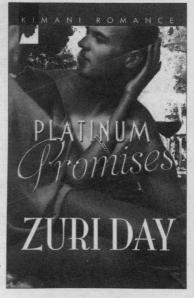

Award-winning wines
have helped Dexter
Drake turn his family's
vineyard into a success
and he is having way too
much fun to settle down.
Until an act of kindness
makes it impossible for
him to get the beautiful Faye Buckner out of his mind. But
will she choose to remain solely focused on her career or
listen to Dexter's passionate promises…and her own heart?

The Drakes of California

"Day's love scenes are fueled by passion and the tale will
keep readers on their toes until the very end."
—*RT Book Reviews* on *DIAMOND DREAMS*

*Available May 2013
wherever books are sold!*

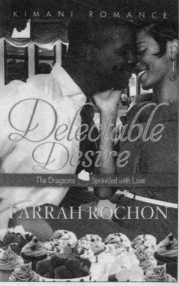

A taste of secret love…

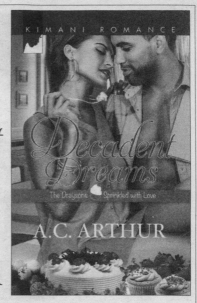

Decadent Dreams

Favorite author
A.C. ARTHUR

Belinda Drayson-Jones is one of the most talented bakers at her family's famed patisserie. Yet perfection has its price, and no one would ever guess the secret she's keeping. But Malik Anthony knows plenty about keeping secrets—he has longed after her for years. And if he's not mistaken, Belinda is now coming on to him. What could be more perfect than giving in?

The Draysons 🧁 Sprinkled with Love

HARLEQUIN®
www.Harlequin.com

Available now wherever books are sold!

KPACA3010413R

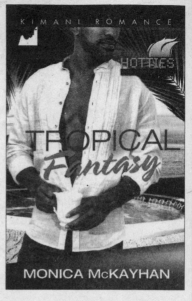